THE HALLOWED ISLE

BOOK THREE:

THE BOOK OF THE CAULDRON

Other Books in
The Hallowed Isle *series by*
Diana L. Paxson

The Book of the Sword
The Book of the Spear

Wodan's Children *Trilogy*

The Dragons of the Rhine
The Wolf and the Raven
The Lord of Horses

With Adrienne Martine-Barnes

Master of Earth and Water
The Shield Between the Worlds
Sword of Fire and Shadow

THE HALLOWED ISLE

BOOK THREE:
THE BOOK OF THE CAULDRON

DIANA L. PAXSON

AVON BOOKS, INC.
1350 Avenue of the Americas
New York, New York 10019

Copyright © 1999 by Diana L. Paxson
Cover illustration by Tom Canty
Interior design by Kellan Peck
Published by arrangement with the author
ISBN: 0-380-80547-2
www.avonbooks.com/eos

Library of Congress Cataloging in Publication Data:

Paxson, Diana L.
    The book of the cauldron / Diana L. Paxson.
        p.   cm. — (The hallowed isle ; bk. 3)
    1. Great Britain—History—Anglo Saxon period, 449–1066 Fiction.
2. Arthurian romances Adaptations. 3. Arthur, King Fiction.
I. Title. II. Series: Paxson, Diana L. Hallowed isle ; bk. 3.
PS3556.A897B64   1999   99-38405
813'.54—dc21   CIP

First Avon Eos Printing: November 1999

AVON EOS TRADEMARK REG. U.S. PAT. OFF. AND IN OTHER COUNTRIES, MARCA REGIS-TRADA, HECHO EN U.S.A.

Printed in the U.S.A.

OPM   10 9 8 7 6 5 4 3 2 1

In Memoriam
Paul Edwin Zimmer

ACKNOWLEDGMENTS

My special thanks to Heather Rose Jones, who took time off from her doctoral studies in Welsh philology to advise me on the mysteries of fifth-century British spelling. For those who would like an excellent historical overview of the Arthurian period, I recommend *The Age of Arthur* by John Morris, recently reprinted by Barnes & Noble. I must also thank Caitlin and John Matthews for some of the insights in their book *Ladies of the Lake*.

Through the fields of European literature, the Matter of Britain flows as a broad and noble stream. In relation to this book especially, a major branch is Marion Zimmer Bradley's *The Mists of Avalon*. Therefore I offer this tributary with thanks and recognition to her and to all those who have gone before.

CONTENTS

PROLOGUE I

I • BIRTH PANGS 3

II • A SHADOW ON THE MOON 20

III • FIRST BLOOD 38

IV • LADY OF THE EASTERN GATE 57

V • THE FLOWER BRIDE 73

VI • THE SACRED ROUND 91

VII • THE WOUNDED KING 106

VIII • THE GREAT QUEEN 126

IX • A VESSEL OF LIGHT 144

X • THE QUEST 159

PEOPLE AND PLACES 176

PROLOGUE

LIFE CAME FIRST FROM THE SEA.

Cradle of creation and sheltering womb, it contained all elements. Dissolved and coalescing, joining, growing, the elements combined to become beings of ascending complexity.

Water is transformation.

Rising and falling, dying and rebirthing, it nourishes the world. Perpetually moving, it obeys the laws of moon and tide. Constrained, it grows stagnant and dies; free flowing, it renews the world.

Water is the blood of the Goddess, flowing through the streams and rivers that vein the land. In the lakes and pools, fed from the depths by bubbling springs, She pours out her blessings.

Water is woman's magic.

As the sea floods in answer to the moon so does her womb; each month she bleeds and is renewed. In blood she creates a child and bloody, she bears it; from her breasts springs sweet milk to be its food. Women seek the sacred spring and make offerings to the Goddess whose name means the power that wells up from the depths to the heights, knowing that her magic and theirs is the same. . . .

On an island in the ocean, nine priestesses serve a sacred shrine. As each moon waxes and wanes they praise the Goddess in Her times and seasons. But often, when the moon is full, the priestess who is their leader walks by the shore of the sea. Moonlight glitters silver on the waters. She stretches out her arms to embrace that splendor, but it flows through her fingers. She aches with yearning to hold the power by which she herself is held, and slowly, within the womb of her head a vision grows.

When the chieftains of her people come to make their offerings she requires of them silver. Piece by piece, she melts it together, beats it out into flat sheets, molded with images of the Goddess. Ready for love or armed for war, healing the sick or giving songs to the bard, milking a cow or hunting a deer or bringing a ship safe to land, nursing her child or bearing the soul of a dead man across the sea, the Goddess appears in all Her guises, blessing humankind.

Section by section the pieces are shaped, riveted and soldered until they are one. From hand and heart a great cauldron is born, silver as the moon. River pearls are set into its rim, gleaming softly. Then, singing, the priestesses bear it to the sacred spring. One by one, each priestess fills her chalice. She lifts it high to catch the radiance of the moon. Then she pours it into the cauldron, shimmering with silver light.

The song grows deeper, becomes a wordless humming, a vibration that shivers the surface of the water. From beyond this world come overtones and harmonies. A mist of radiance glows above the water, twines upward, shapes itself into the form of a woman. Turning, She opens her arms, Her voice joins in the singing, and shapes it into words. She dips liquid from the cauldron; into each chalice She pours Her blessings, and all are filled.

And when at last, the priestesses return to awareness of who and where they are, the Cauldron is empty. But every full moon when they fill it with water from the sacred spring, that water glows, and all who drink of it are renewed.

BIRTH PANGS

A·D· 487

JUST BEFORE SUNSET, A WIND CAME DOWN FROM THE HEIGHTS to ruffle the water. The Lady of the Lake breathed it in gratefully, for the day had been warm, a promise of the summer season that Beltain would usher in. In the lands of men, the young folk would be going out into the woods to gather greenery for the festival, and if they took rather longer than was strictly necessary to cut the branches, and came back with their clothing awry, even the Christians would hardly dare chastise them on this eve. But on the Isle of Maidens there was no need to bring in the wilderness, for it was all around them. And while man and maid performed the old earth magic, she and her priestesses would invoke the magic of the waters whose power enabled all these green and growing things to survive.

Beyond the screen of willow and the silver sheen of the water, the mountain crouched like an old woman, cloaked and hooded in misty blue, hunched against the dimming sky. Igierne had seen it so when, as a girl, she first claimed this spot as her private bathing place. Now she was an old woman herself. But the mountain remained the same.

She hung the rough towel across a branch and slid the cloak

3

from around her shoulders, shivering a little at the touch of the air. For a moment she hesitated to remove her shift as well, but it was not going to get any warmer. Lips twisting wryly, she dragged it over her head and made her way down to the waterside.

White and wavering as a birch trunk, she saw her body reflected there. *I am a waning moon* ... she thought wryly. Even her hair, once golden, was faded now to silver-fair. As a girl, she had spied on the older priestesses at their bathing and been astonished to find their bodies still so smooth. It surprised her still, looking down, to see her own shape so much younger than the face in her mirror. True, her breasts lay pendant upon her ribcage, and her belly had been stretched by the weight of two children, but her buttocks were round with muscle from walking, and her arms were firm.

If Uthir had been living, she would have rejoiced in his delight in her body, but he slept now beside his brother in the mound before the Giant's Dance. No longer was she high queen and his lady. Now it was her son Artor who ruled. When the princes of Britannia chose him, Igierne had offered to stay and manage his household, but the lords of Britannia, having accepted her son's right to rule them, wanted no motherly meddling in the process of turning him into a king. Even Merlin had been tolerated only grudgingly as his tutor, perhaps because they feared him.

And so she had returned to the Isle of Maidens to reclaim the role for which she had been born. She wrote to Artor with some regularity, seeking to supply the guidance she had not been allowed to give before, but increasingly her counsel came from her meditations as a priestess, rather than her memories of life as Uthir's queen. On the rare occasions when she visited her son, his court seemed like another world. These days, the health of her body mattered only because it served her soul. And that—she smiled down at the woman who looked back at her from the water—was still that of the maiden who had first bathed in these waters so long ago.

Still smiling, she stepped down the shelving strand into the water.

"Blessed be my feet, that I may walk in Thy ways ...

blessed be my legs, that I may stand before Thee . . . blessed be my womb, that I may be Thy shrine . . ." She scooped up water, purifying each part of her body, murmuring the words that would make her a fit vessel for the power of the Goddess to fill.

The Isle of Maidens lay hidden within the double enclosure of the Lake and its encircling hills. The Romans had massacred the Druid priesthood on the isle of Mona, and driven them from Afallon that men now called the Isle of Glass, but this sanctuary they had never found. In time its huts of daubed withies had been replaced by stone, but in some things the priestesses still held by the old Druid ways, and the most sacred of their rituals took place beneath the open sky.

If the island was doubly warded, the hazelwood formed the innermost barrier around its center, where a fissure in the island's rocky core had created a cave. The Sword-God's shrine had been a temple built by men, tolerated, but never truly belonging to the isle. The cave was its most ancient and original sanctuary. Three fires burned now before it, but the entrance remained in shadow.

Igierne lay back against the carved wood of her chair, willing her breathing to remain steady, waiting for her heartbeat to slow. Her pale hair lay loose upon her shoulders. For this ceremony her maidens were robed in white. Only she wore the black of the midnight sky, though her ornaments were of silver, set with moonstone and river pearls.

Overhead, a scattering of stars glimmered in the river of night. Long practice had taught her to sense the slow turning of the skies. The moon was in its third quarter, and would not rise till the night was half gone. Imperceptibly her breathing began to deepen. She straightened, hearing her own heartbeat echoed by the soft beat of a drum. Anticipation tightened her skin as the women began to sing—

"Thou art the source and the stream . . .
Thou art the desire and the dream . . .

that which is empty and that which fills,
that which receives and that which wills;
Thou art the part and Thou art the whole,
Thou art the body and Thou, the soul. . . . "

The mingled voices converged in a single note, sustained in a long vibration that thrummed in the still air. Elsewhere they called on the gods in other guises, and by other names, especially on this night, when the young God came forth from his leafy glades to couple with the Goddess in the fields. But here, at the heart of the isle, it was the Lady alone who ruled.

"Great Mother, be near us—" intoned Igierne.

"Hear us, be near us . . ." came the reply.

"Gateway to birth and doorway to death—" Ceincair's sweet voice rose above the rest.

"Hear us. . . ."

"Lady of hope and healing—" the litany went on, and with each salutation, the air seemed to thicken until it was difficult to breathe.

"Thou art the Cauldron of Changes, the Womb of Wisdom—" said Igierne, and at her words, Morut and Nest moved to the dark opening of the cave and began to pull the stones away. Beneath them was a wooden chest carved with triple spirals, and within the chest, something swathed in white silk which they set in the hollow of the stone before Igierne's chair.

As the cloth fell away, she felt her awareness shifting so that she saw with doubled vision the ancient cauldron of riveted silver plates on which goddess-faces and the images of strange beasts stood out in low relief, and a vessel of pure Light, outshining the fires.

A white-clad shape moved forward. From a silver pitcher, water poured into the cauldron in a glistening stream. The light grew brighter.

"I bring water from the ocean, the womb of the world. Receive the offering!" the voice was that of Nest.

Another moved into the radiance. "I bring water from the

Tamesis, lifeblood of the land—" More water glittered through the air.

One by one the priestesses emptied their pitchers. The water they offered came from each of the great rivers that drained Britannia, and from the sacred springs.

"I bring water from the Isle of Mona . . ." chanted Morut.

"I bring water from the blood spring of Afallon . . ." sang Ceincair.

The light grew; glowing figures moved within a bright haze. Igierne stared into the glimmering depths of the Cauldron.

"Speak to us, Lady, " she whispered. "In this moment when the doors open between the worlds, show us what is to be. . . ."

With that prayer, all other awareness became peripheral. The light welled up around her and she was free.

She saw Britannia laid out below her, picked out in lines of light as one Beltain fire signaled another across the land. Disciplines practiced for so long they had become instinct turned her mind toward those whose future she must see.

Beltain fires blazed on the hills above Isca. Igierne's gaze followed the flicker of light and shadow as men and women danced around them. Her son Artor was there, with Betiver and Cai, and that odd Saxon boy who they said was Hengest's grandson. Girls came to the king, laughing, and he kissed them and drank the mead they offered, but though many of his men allowed themselves to be led off into the leafy shadows, and Gualchmai was no doubt there already, Artor remained by the fires.

Is this how you honor the Goddess, my child? Igierne thought ruefully, and heard, as if in agreement, a ripple of silvery laughter. But Artor had grown up suspecting himself a bastard, she remembered with sudden pain. No wonder if he took care where he sowed his own seed.

He must have a queen to act as your priestess, Lady! she told the bright darkness. *Show me the woman who will share his bed and his throne!*

The image shattered. Colors ran in swirls of liquid light, painting a land of folded hills and peaceful woodlands, altogether a gentler country than the Demetian shore. In a sheltered valley the villa of a British prince lay dark while his tribesmen revelled in the meadow below. But at the edge of the firelight something stirred. Igierne's vision focused; she saw a slim girl-child with amber eyes and a cloud of red-gold hair clutching an old blanket around her as she watched the dancing. Even standing, she seemed to sway like a young tree in the wind. She would be beautiful in motion.

As the image dimmed, the Voice of the Goddess sounded in Igierne's awareness once more—"*She is Leodagranus' daughter. Her name is Guendivar...*"

She is young, yet, thought Igierne, *too young to understand what this means, I must find her and prepare her for her destiny.*

Images flickered before her: Guendivar grown, her bright hair crowned with flowers ... laughing, dancing, racing through the woods on a grey dappled mare ... and older still, her face racked by grief and looking for the first time like that of a mortal woman and not a maiden of faerie. Igierne strove to see more, but the vision became a blur that left her dazed and dizzy, floating in the void.

With an effort she regained her focus. To foresee fate did not necessarily show one how to change it, for the ancients held that it was always changing, and in seeking to avoid the end foretold many a man had instead been its cause. Better to seek knowledge of events nearer to hand, so that one might, if not prevent, at least prepare to meet them.

Morgause ... With a regretful recognition that her concern sprang more from duty than desire, Igierne sought to see the outcome of her daughter's pregnancy.

On the height of Dun Eidyn the Votadini warriors drank to their king. She saw Morgause bearing the horn among them, too heavily pregnant for dancing. From time to time she would pause, biting her lip for a moment before continuing her round.

The child will come very soon, thought Igierne, *does she know it?* But this was Morgause's fifth pregnancy. She must know her own body's signals by now. It was stubbornness, not ignorance, that kept her on her feet this Beltain Eve. Igierne suppressed the irritation that thoughts of her daughter too often inspired.

Will the birthing go well? What will this child bring to Britannia?

Vision was dazzled by the blaze of morning light on water. But in the next moment a tide of red replaced it. A child's angry wail deepened into the battlefield roar of an army. Fear for her daughter gave way to a deeper terror as she saw Morgause, her features sagging with middle age and twisted by hatred, and beside her, a boy whose features were a younger, fairer, reflection of her own, with a hint of someone else in the line of the jaw that Igierne could not quite recognize. Was it that which set something deep within to shivering, or was it the spark of malice in his eyes? Red darkness swirled across her vision: a raven banner tossed against a fiery sky. And then it was a flight of ravens, and a Voice that cried—

"He shall bring blood and fire and the end of an age . . . All things pass, else lack of balance would destroy the world."

Igierne writhed in soundless repudiation, knowing, even as she hated it, that this Voice also was divine. And then, like cool water, the Goddess as she had always known Her spoke in her soul.

"Fear not. While the ravens ward the White Mount, the Guardian of Britannia will remain. . . ."

She felt herself falling back into her body, starlight and firelight and the light of her visions shattering around her like a mosaic of Roman glass. Desperately she tried to fix the pieces in some pattern that would retain its meaning, but they were moving too fast.

"Merlin!" her soul cried, *"Merlin, hear me! Beware the child that is born the first of May!"*

Then it was over, though she ached in every limb. Igierne felt soft hands helping her to sit upright, heard a murmur of shock and concern.

"My lady, are you all right?"

"I will be . . ." she muttered. *Artor—* she thought, *I must speak with him soon.* Then she took a deep breath and opened her eyes to see the gibbous quarter-moon staring down at her from a sky that was already paling before the first light of Beltain's dawn.

At dawn on Beltain, Morgause went out with her women to bring water from the sacred spring. Before sunrise the air was brisk and Morgause was glad of the fleecy cloak she wore. Unbalanced by the great bulge of her belly, she moved carefully, picking her way down the rocky path in the uncertain torchlight and the light of the waning moon that was more deceptive still. From the group of maidens who walked with her came laughter, swiftly hushed. The child in her belly stirred, then stilled. Perhaps, she thought hopefully, the unaccustomed motion would lull him to sleep. He had kept her wakeful half the night with his kicking, as if he could not wait for the womb to open and set him free.

To walk from the fortress down to the base of the cleft below it and back could take half the morning, and the return climb required considerable stamina. The women, eyeing the queen's distended belly, had begged her to let one of the chieftains' daughters who attended her represent her in the ceremony, but Morgause refused. For a girl to take her place in Leudonus' bed during her pregnancies did not threaten her position, but her condition had not permitted her to dance at the Beltain fires. Morgause would allow no one to usurp any of the other sacred duties of the queen.

"It will be safe enough," she told them. "The babe is not due for another half moon." This was not quite true—she knew very well that this child had been conceived in the rites at the feast of Lugus, and so her pregnancy was now full term. But her other children had come behind time, so she told the lie without compunction.

Men might speculate, when the queen's sons were born some nine moons after a festival, but those who did not follow the old ways could never be certain they were not of Leudonus' begetting. The majority of the Votadini tribesmen believed, like Morgause, that her children were a gift from the gods.

For a moment vision blurred; the torchlit darkness of the road became the festival ground, and the chill of dawn the warm summer night of Lughnasaid. The people were shouting, a hero came to her in the darkness of the sacred enclosure, filled with the god, and then the dark fire of the goddess reft her own awareness away . . .

Morgause trembled again, remembering. It was only afterwards, listening to folk speak of the bull-fight and how the young king from the south had saved the fallen priest of Lugus and completed the ceremony, that she understood that it was Artor who had lain in her arms.

She had considered, in that moment of realization, seeking out the herbs that would cast the child from her womb. But the gods had willed that her brother's seed take root there. She did not dare deny them. Morgause was built for bearing, but a woman offered her life in childbed as a man marched into battle. Soon, now, the gods would judge both mother and child. And if such a child lived . . . surely he was meant for a mighty destiny.

A stone turned under her foot and she grasped at the arm of Dugech, who walked beside her.

"Lady, please, let me send for a litter to take you back to the dun!"

Morgause shook her head. To give up now would be an admission of weakness. She straightened defiantly.

"Then let us carry you down—"

Morgause started forward again without answering. The sky was growing lighter. The far side of the cleft stood in stark outline against that pallor; a gulf of darkness gaped below. *I am descending into the Underworld,* she thought, suppressing panic. For a moment she considered letting Dugech have her way, but now that the exercise had got her blood running, she felt better than she had before.

"The rite requires that I walk to the spring, and it will do me good. I have sat too long indoors. Only stay close so that I do not fall."

They moved on. The pallor above brightened to a pearly grey, and then, as the torch flames grew pale and the shapeless masses of shadow that edged the path became shrubs and trees lightened, with a hint of rose. They had reached the crossroads where the way that ran down the vale crossed the path that descended from the dun. Morgause turned. Behind the jagged peak of the Watch Hill the sky was beginning to flame with gold.

She tried to hurry then, ignoring the slow ache across her lower back. She wished now that she had called for the litter, but she had almost reached the spring. With relief she felt the pathway level out and took a deep breath of moist air. Beneath their mantles the white linen garments of her maidens glowed. Morgause paused to undo the pins that held her own cloak and straightened gratefully as its weight slithered to the ground. The flesh on her arms pebbled at the touch of the brisk air, but her blood was still heated from the walk and she did not mind the cold.

She beckoned to red-haired Leuku, who was carrying the bronze vessel, and strode toward the spring. To the east the sky was bright gold. Overhead the heavens glowed pale rose, but the scattered clouds, catching the sunlight, had hung out banners of flame.

The women stood in silence, watching that radiance intensify until the rock above was edged with a sliver of flame. As the sunwheel rolled up the sky, light blazed between the birches and sparkled on the waters of the well as if a fire had been kindled within. Pent breath was released in a shout—

"Water of life from the depths upwelling—" sang the queen.

"Bring us thy blessing!" her maidens chorused in reply.

"Fire of power from the heavens descending—"

"Bring us thy blessing!"

"Fire in the water kindling cool flame—" she sang then, and waited for the others to reply.

"Power we drink and protection we claim."

Carefully, she bent and tipped the rim of the kettle so that the glittering water trickled in. As she began to stand up, the ache across her loins became a sudden pang. For a moment Morgause could not move. When she could breathe again, she straightened, telling herself it had only been another preliminary pain. She had been having them for weeks, and knew them for the distant thunder that heralds the storm.

But with her next step, Morgause felt a trickle of warm fluid between her thighs, and understood that the time of waiting was done.

"My lady!" cried Dugech as the gush soaked the back of the queen's gown.

Morgause managed a smile. "The waters of my womb flow like those of the holy well. Let them be my offering. . . ." She held out the cauldron, and Leuku, her eyes wide, took it from her hands.

Without waiting for orders, Dugech whispered to one of the younger girls and sent her sprinting back up the trail.

"Let us spread our mantles to make a bed for you, lady, and you can lie down until the litter arrives."

Morgause shook her head. "I walked half the night to bear my first child. This labor will go easier if I get as far as I can under my own power." She knew that she was challenging the gods, but so long as she was moving, she could maintain the illusion that this process was under her control. Ignoring the shocked protest of the maidens, she started back along the trail.

From time to time a pain overwhelmed her and she would pause, gripping Dugech's shoulder until it passed. But it soon became apparent that this child was in a hurry to come into the world. By the time they reached the crossroads, the pains were coming swiftly. Morgause swayed, dragging in breath in hoarse gasps. The women were piling their cloaks on the grass beside the road. Dugech took one arm and Leuku the other, and Morgause could no longer resist them. Biting her lip against the pain, she let them help her down to lie with her back braced against the bank where the pale primroses grew.

Her fingers clenched in the new grass as the muscles of her belly contracted and released again. She was aware that the litter had arrived, but by then things had gone too far for her to be moved.

She fixed her gaze on the hollow moon, sliding down the western sky like a rind of pearl. She could hear the girls whispering. It was not right that the queen of the Votadini should give birth like a beggar woman beside the road. And at a crossroads too! At Beltain, when the folk of faerie moved from their winter quarters to their summer homes, more might be passing along that road than men. Morgause shook her head, denying her own fear. This pregnancy itself had been a challenge to the gods—it should be no surprise that the birth was the same.

"Draw the circle of safety around me if you are afraid—" she grunted between pangs, "and then get ready to catch the babe."

The muscles of her belly writhed again, and she was unable to suppress a groan. Between birthings one always forgot the pain, but it seemed to her that the violence of the pangs that tore her now was greater than any she had known, as if the womb were trying to turn itself inside out in its haste to expel the weight it bore.

"Mother . . ." she whimpered, and then bit back the word. Blood trickled from between her thighs to stain the crimson gown. Igierne was not there—had never been there, really, when Morgause needed her, even when they were living in the same hall. Why should she call for her now?

Morgause had always taken such pride in her ability to bear sons. But women died in childbirth, and she was no longer in her first youth. *Am I dying?* Her thoughts circled in confusion. *Is the Goddess claiming my offering?* Shadows danced before her eyes like dark wings.

I am in Your hands, Lady . . . I offer my life if it will serve you, and that of my child. She let out her breath in a long sigh, feeling a dim sorrow, but no fear.

Then another convulsion took her and she cried out once more. The rolling ache became a wrenching agony.

"Warrior, and mother of warriors—now you shall fight for your life!" came a voice from within. *"Cast the babe from your body, now!"*

Morgause drew up her legs and dug her heels into the soft earth and pushed with all the strength she had. The pressure increased, as if she were being split in two. Again her muscles clenched and she bore down. She felt the gush of birthblood and a burning pain in her sex as the child's head crowned. Against her closed eyelids the sunlight was a whirl of red brightness. She sucked in air, and then with the last of her strength, pushed once more.

There was a moment of pulsing relief as the babe slid, warm and slippery, between her thighs. She gasped for breath, and in echo, heard his furious challenge to the world. The babe was still yelling when Dugech tied off and cut the cord and laid him on her breast.

Morgause lay in drowsy stupor, the contractions of the birth fading from her wracked body like the last tremors of love. She felt the warm seep of blood from her womb sinking into the thirsty soil and found it hard to care. Anxious voices twittered around her, but she ignored them. Only when hard fingers began to knead her belly did she open her eyes with a weak cry.

"My lady, the afterbirth must be driven forth—" said Leuku as the queen protested. The baby was still squalling.

"Set the child to the teat," someone said then.

There were a few moments of confusion as they undid her gown. Morgause felt the babe rootling at her breast, and then a sudden sharp pang that shocked through her entire body as he fastened onto the nipple and her milk let down. Through the convulsions that followed as she was delivered of the placenta he hung on. It was only when he let go at last that she saw blood flowing from her nipple along with the milk and realized that her son had been born toothed and ready to take on the world.

From nearby came the deep rumble of male voices. Morgause looked up and saw Leudonus' grizzled head above the others.

"You have a fine son, my lord, for all that he came early into the world—" said Dugech, leading the king into the circle of women. Morgause's lips twitched as the other woman bent to take the swaddled child from her arms.

Dugech knew perfectly well that this boy, like the others, was full-term. Even Leudonus, who had sired his share of bastards, must know the difference by now, but if so, he had his own reasons to uphold the fiction. He frowned down at the squirming bundle Dugech had handed him, and silence fell while men waited for him to acknowledge paternity.

"A fine boy indeed. He has your hair," he said finally. And then, holding him up, "Let him be called Medraut, of the royal kindred. Let the Votadini welcome a future warrior!"

This, if not explicit, was close enough to an avowal. The walls of the cleft echoed to their shout of welcome. Morgause smiled. *A warrior*, she thought, *and more than a warrior. I welcome a king!* She could sleep now, knowing others would guard her child. The moon had finally disappeared, but through her closing eyelids, she still saw the red glow of the Beltain Sun.

If she slitted her eyes just so, thought Guendivar, the reflections from the warriors' spearpoints merged into a single dazzle of light. That was almost more fun than watching them throw the spears, and certainly better than listening to them argue about the casts. She had promised Telent that she would watch him compete today. He was in Prince Leodagranus' guard, and carried her around on his shoulders, though the last time she asked he had said that at almost seven, she was too old.

Guendivar chewed on her lower lip, watching as he prepared to cast anew. She knew that she was growing, but he was *very* tall. Perhaps she would go away now, to punish him.

At the thought, she was already in motion, flitting past the line of men like a white blossom before the wind. Her mother, who had been dozing in the shade of the figured cloth, sat up suddenly, calling, but by then Guendivar was halfway down the field and could pretend she had not heard. Petronilla was always trying to make her be polite and tidy; Guendivar had learned the advantages of evasion early on.

She wanted to see the rest of the festival. At the edge of the field, peddlers had set up their wares in bothies made of woven branches and strips of striped cloth. There were only a few, and their goods would have been considered paltry stuff when the Romans ruled, but only the older people remembered those days. In the old days they would probably have celebrated the festival in Lindinis, her father's town, instead of spending most of their time at the old villa in the hills. To the folk of the countryside, the red pottery oil lamps and the beads of Roman glass seemed very fine. Guendivar wandered among them, admiring, and one of the traders gave her a green ribbon to tie back her hair.

The afternoon was waning when she saw one of her mother's women advancing toward her with a decidedly repressive look in her eye. Rather suddenly Guendivar remembered that Petronilla had been quite explicit about the behavior that was expected of a chieftain's daughter at this festival. She knew that she had disobeyed, and she did not mind being punished once it was over, but the sun was still well above the trees!

Before the woman could grab her, Guendivar was off again, slipping behind a cart and then around the horse-lines and toward the protection of the trees. Perhaps her father's huntsmen knew these woods better than she did, but Guendivar did not think anyone else could find her once she was among the trees. And even a woodsman might think twice about entering the tunnels that a small girl could negotiate with ease.

One of them brought her out into a small glade surrounded by hazels. The grass in the center was flattened, as if someone had been sleeping there, and hanging on one of the hazel twigs was a flower crown. Guendivar began to smile.

To watch the dancing last night had been exciting, with the drumming and the naked bodies shining in the light of the fires. She had not quite understood what those men and girls were seeking when they leaped over the flames or ran, half-embraced and laughing, for the forest, but she knew it must be something wonderful, part of the magic she felt pulsing from the land itself on Beltain eve.

Guendivar could still sense it, a little, here in the glade. She sat still, senses extended, feeling the warmth of the afternoon radiating from the grass. The sounds of the festival seemed distant, and as she continued to sit and her eyelids grew heavy, more distant still. She had not gotten much sleep the night before, and the day had been busy. The warm air caressed her and she curled drowsily down into the tangled grass.

*   *   *

It was the change in the light that roused her, a ray of the sinking sun that found its way through the tangle of branches to her closed eyelids. Still half-asleep, she scrunched them shut more tightly and turned her head, but the sun's angle let the last of its radiance pour through the trees. Sighing, Guendivar rubbed her eyes and slitted them open.

Within the glade, every stock and stone was glowing, and each leaf and blade of grass was edged with flame. *Pretty . . .* she thought, watching with half-focused gaze, and stretched out her arm. *Everything has light inside, even me. . . .* Beneath the scratches and the smears of soil and the scattering of golden freckles, her pale flesh shone.

A flicker at the edge of vision caught her attention. Her vision refocused; something was moving there. Bemused by beauty, she did not stir, even when her vision transmuted the spiraling sparkles into attenuated figures that danced and darted about the glade. At first they seemed tiny, but they seemed able to change their size at will, and they moved as if weightless, or winged. And presently she realized that su-surrus of sound was neither the wind nor music, but the chatter of high, sweet voices.

Fragments of old tales configured themselves into sudden certainty. Slowly Guendivar sat up, refusing to blink, lest the vision flicker away.

"I know you now . . ." she said softly. "You are faerie-folk. Have you just moved house into these woods today?"

For a moment even the motes of light seemed to stop moving. Then the air shimmered with faerie laughter.

"She sees us! She can see!" The faeries clustered around her in a glowing swirl. One of the figures floated upward to face her, expanding until it was as large as a child of three.

"Of course I can see you," answered Guendivar. "I have seen faeries before, I think," she added, remembering, "but they never talked to me."

"It is the moment between day and darkness, and in this child, the old blood runs true," said one of the others. *"But she will lose the vision when she is grown."*

Guendivar glared, but a new question was already on her lips. "Will you show me your country?"

"*This* is *our country—it is all around you, if you have the eyes to see—*" came the answer, and indeed, when Guendivar lifted her eyes, the familiar shapes of tree and rock seemed doorways to unguessed dimensions. But she dared not look too long, for fear that her new friends would flit away.

"Then will you give me a wish?" she asked.

"*Our gifts can be dangerous . . .*" the faerie responded, but Guendivar only laughed.

"Am I in danger here?" She grinned. "My wish is that my heart shall stay as it is now, and I shall always be able to see faerie."

"*Are you certain? Folk so sighted may find it difficult to live in the mortal world. . . .*"

Guendivar shrugged. "I think it is boring already. It will not matter to me."

"*It will matter . . .*" said the faerie, with momentary sadness. Then it, too, laughed. "*But we cannot refuse you on this day.*"

Guendivar clapped her hands, and as if on cue, the sun slid behind the hilltop and the light was gone. Her new friends were gone, too. For a moment she felt like crying, but it was getting cold, and she was hungry. She looked for the tunnel through the hazels, and found that to her altered vision, the world around her still shone from within.

The faerie had not lied to her. Laughing once more, Guendivar ran back to the world of humankind.

II

A SHADOW ON THE MOON

A.D. 489

JUST AT DUSK, ON AN EVENING WHEN THE FIRST SLIVER OF THE first new moon of summer hung above the brow of the hill, Merlin arrived at the Lake. As always, he came alone and unheralded, appearing like a spirit at the edge of the forest. Igierne, on her way to the rock at the highest point of the island for her evening meditation, felt his presence like a breath of scent, which at first teases, and then releases a flood of memories. She stopped short on the path, so that Morut nearly ran into her.

"Go down to the landing and send the boat across to the shore. We have a visitor."

Morut's eyes widened, but she did not question Igierne's knowledge. Smiling, Igierne watched her go.

When she had first returned to the Lake to reclaim her role as its Lady, after Artor was made king, Igierne had felt herself half an impostor. The skills required of a bean-drui needed focus, application, constant honing. She was like a warrior taking down the sword he has allowed to rust on the wall. And yet her mental muscles, though stiff and clumsy, still remembered their early training, and in time she found that the passing years had given her a depth of understanding that had not been there when she was a girl. There might be others on the island to whom these skills came more easily, but none with her judgment regarding how and when they should be used. And after a dozen years as Tigernissa of Britain, Igierne found it easy to rule a gaggle of women and girls.

But Merlin, she thought as she watched him coming towards her, had wisdom of a different and higher order still. When she was a young woman, he had seemed much older than she, but from the vantage of fifty-two, a man in his early sixties was a contemporary. It was not age that set him so apart from other men, but an inherent wildness, despite all his years in the courts of kings.

He wore his accustomed wolfskin over a druid's white gown. Both were well-worn, as if they had grown to his gaunt frame. But he looked strong. Later, as she poured mint tea into his bowl from the kettle that steamed over her fire, she realized that Merlin was assessing her as well.

"I am no longer the girl you knew in Luguvalium . . ." she said softly.

"You are still beautiful—" he answered her thought rather than her words "—as the forest in autumn, when the nuts ripen on the trees."

Igierne felt herself flushing, and shook her head. "My moon has passed the full, but it is the sun we should be speaking of. When did you last see Artor?"

Merlin raised one bushy eyebrow in gentle mockery, but allowed her self-deprecation to pass. "Two, or nearly three moons past. He is rebuilding the fort at Isca. Castra Legionis, they call it. It will serve as a staging area for campaigns against raiders from Eriu. It was very crowded and full of soldiers. I did not stay long."

"That is the main threat, then? Not the Saxons?"

The druid shrugged. "At present. Artor has tamed Hengest's cub and set him to guard the sheep in Cantium, but the rest of the Saxon pack are still hungry. Ceretic sits in Venta, licking his chops and eyeing the lands around him, and the Anglians roam the fens. Artor will have to deal with them eventually. But why do you ask me? Does not he write to you?"

"From time to time—" She tapped the carved wooden casket where she kept Artor's letters. "But a druid's sight is different from that of a king."

"I cannot rule for him, Igierne," Merlin answered her, "nor can you."

She frowned, thinking of the advice she had been sending. Someone must speak for the Goddess, until Artor had a queen. "Is that why you spend so much time roaming the wilds?" she countered. "What if something happens? What if he needs you?"

"I will know." His voice was a subterranean rumble, as if he spoke thorough stone. "The stars have shown me that a crisis is coming. For good or for ill, it will settle things with the Saxons for a generation. When that time comes, it is ordained that I be there."

Igierne felt the truth of that in her bones. For a few moments there was no sound but the hiss of the fire.

"I too have searched the future," she said finally. "Two years ago, at Beltain. This year I dared not—I was afraid. I remember the terror, but of what I saw I know only that the Lady of Ravens was there, and red war coming, and a child."

"I know Her . . ." Merlin's face twisted with ancient sorrow. "Only the White Raven can stand against her when the war horns blow."

"But what of the child?"

"You called out to me in that vision, and I heard—" Merlin threw up his hands in exasperation. "But what would you have me do? Should I have counselled Artor to order every child born on the first of May exposed? Even Caesar would have been unable to enforce such a decree! Foreknowledge is a deceptive gift, Igierne, for our hopes and fears distort the shapes of what we see. When I was young I searched the heavens constantly, but the older I get, the less I seek to know."

"But if you foresee a danger, you can avoid it—" she exclaimed.

"Can you? The Greeks tell of a man called Oedipus, whose efforts to flee his fate instead fulfilled it."

Igierne glared at him. She knew that as women got older

they often became stronger, more resolute, while many men grew gentler in old age. Certainly it was so with Merlin. He, who in their young days had been hard as the hills, seemed now as elusive as wind or water.

"If I see danger coming to my country or my child I will confront it," she told him, leaning forward with her hands on her knees. "And I will not cease to fight that fate while life shall last."

"Perhaps that is *your* fate, Igierne," Merlin said gently, and smiled.

"Mother, Aggarban is wearing my red belt!"

"Why can't I have it? You said you weren't taking it with you—"

Gwyhir's reply was muffled, as if he had decided to take matters into his own hands. Morgause sighed. She had been regretting Leudonus' decision to send her second son to join his brother at the court of Artor, but just at this moment she did not care whether he went to Castra Legionis or the Devil, if she could have peace in her house once more.

"Let him have it, Gwyhir," she snapped, thrusting aside the curtain between her closet-bed and the central common area around the fire. "You were telling me only yesterday that the belt is too small."

"But he should *ask*, mother," said Gwyhir, straightening to his full height. He had got man-high in the past moons, but was still growing into his bones. His hair, lighter than Gualchmai's, stuck out at odd angles, giving him the look of a young bird.

Aggarban still wore the belt, though he was flushed and rumpled where his brother had grabbed him. He was dark and stocky, not much taller than the fourth brother, Goriat, even though he was almost four years older. Morgause looked at them and shook her head. She was too young to be the mother of such a brood of big, boisterous boys. At the moment, she wanted to send them *all* to Artor; all, that is, except for her sweet Medraut.

Her youngest son was turned two this spring. She had danced at the Beltain fires this year and gone into the woods afterwards with one of Leudonus' warriors. But she had not kindled. She told herself it meant nothing—there were three years between Gwyhir and Aggarban, after all, and four between Goriat and Medraut—but in her heart the fear was growing that Medraut would be her last child. Was he her punishment, or her key to greatness? She still did not know.

"Will you write and tell us all about Artor's fortress?" asked Goriat.

"I will be far too busy to write letters," answered his brother loftily, "riding, and training with the sword and spear. When I win my first fight I will let you know."

"And what if you lose?" Aggarban stuck out his tongue and darted out of the way of his brother's blow.

"Our brother Gualchmai is the greatest warrior the High King has," said Gwyhir. "He may beat me, but by the gods, nobody else will, once my training is done."

At least, thought his mother, he recognized that he still had a few things to learn. But in the long run, she shared his confidence. No son of hers could be anything but a champion.

"A fine lad," said Bliesbituth as they watched Gwyhir ride out with Leudonus and his men. He was a chieftain who often served as a courier between Fodreu and Dun Eidyn. "But why do you send him to the Romans? If you let him come to Pictland, we would marry him to one of our princesses and he might father kings." He smiled at his wife, a plump, pretty woman called Tulach, who was herself of the royal lineage.

"I have several sons," Morgause said diplomatically. "Perhaps one of the others—"

"You think I am flattering," said Bliesbituth, "but it is not so. Britannia was strong in the time of the emperors, but their time is ended. The Votadini should look northward. We were never conquered; our warriors never gave up their swords. If all the peoples who live north of the Wall were to unite, we would be a power to reckon with. The Romans call us the Picts, the painted people, but we are the Pretani, the true Britons of this isle. The south is exhausted—our time is coming now."

Morgause felt the blood of generations who had fought to

defend that Wall burning in her cheeks, but she held her tongue. From all accounts, Artor was keeping the Saxons and the men of Eriu in check; she was too tactful to remind Bliesbituth how her brother had dealt with the Picts three years before. The Romans, even at the height of their power, had been able to do little more.

Another thought chilled her suddenly. If all the might of Rome had been able to do no better, what did that say about the power of Alba? While Artor was young and strong, perhaps he could hold the north in check, but what about his successor? The lords of Britannia had refused to make her husband their king because his power was too far from the center of things, but in the time that was coming, it might be that only a king whose strength lay on the borders could hope to rule. *A king like my son . . .* she thought, smiling grimly, *my Medraut. . . .*

"And there is this to think on," said Tulach. "They say that the people of the south have abandoned their gods. The new religion teaches love, and peace. Is it any wonder that the empire has fallen? You think you keep the old ways here, my queen, but among the Pretani we have preserved the ancient traditions in all their purity. It is not only our menfolk who have power!" The silver ornaments clasped in the tight curls of her bronze brown hair chimed softly as she nodded.

Morgause smiled thinly. "It is true that there are many in Britannia who follow the Christos, but I am the daughter of the Lady of the Lake and the heir to its mysteries."

"No doubt, but there are things we could teach you, Morgause."

Morgause did not answer her. The dust of Leudonus' cavalcade was fading, and it was time to go in. She could not deny that for a moment Tulach's offer had tempted her. But the power that waited on the Isle of Maidens was bred in her, blood and bone. It had been too long since she had tasted its waters and breathed its air.

She should pay her mother a visit, she thought then, and take Medraut. It was time Igierne met her youngest grandchild.

*   *   *

"Well, Morgause, motherhood certainly agrees with you. You are blooming like a rose!" Ebrdila grinned toothlessly and patted the bench beside her. Behind her, the roses in Igierne's garden had been trained over an arbor. In this sheltered spot, the red blooms clustered in profusion, scattering bright petals upon the path.

True, thought Igierne, surveying her daughter with a more critical eye, *but this rose is beginning to look just a bit blown.*

Morgause still had a fine, full figure, but after five children, her breasts no longer rode high, and the muscles of her belly had not yet recovered their tone. But it was her face that had prompted the observation, as Igierne noted the permanent high color in the cheeks, and around the mouth, the first faint lines of discontent. Ebrdila's old eyes might not be able to see it—but then Morgause had been her special pet since the days when Igierne, newly married to Uthir, had left the girl in her care.

"Oh, I am very well!" Morgause gave the old woman a swift hug as she sat down beside her, "and so is my baby. Is he not a fine boy?" She smiled complacently at the child who was playing with the rose petals in the path.

"He is indeed," answered Ebrdila, "just like his mother!"

Igierne had to admit the boy was handsome, though most children, however ugly as babies or gawky as they grew, were plump and rosy at this age. Had Artor been so sweetly rounded when he was two, so seriously intent upon the wonders of the world? Regret for the lost years ached like an old wound in her breast. This boy's hair shone like burnished bronze in the sunlight—Morgause had been the same—but when he looked up, Igierne found herself disconcerted by his considering stare. Then he grabbed for another rose petal and laughed, and the odd moment was gone.

Igierne cleared her throat. "And how is Leudonus?" For a moment Morgause simply stared at her. *Your husband,* thought Igierne, *surely you remember him, even if he is not the father of this child.*

"He is in Isca with Artor," Morgause answered, a little defiantly. "He took Gwyhir into his household with Gualchmai. But surely you knew that—do not you and your son correspond? I thought he asked your advice every time he wiped—"

"Morgause!" Ebrdila chided gently, "There is no need to be coarse."

She had not criticized the content of the remark, only its expression. But at least Igierne now knew that the jealousy Morgause had felt for her brother when she was a girl was still there.

"And did Leudonus suggest that you spend his absence here?" she asked, trying to keep her tone from becoming sarcastic. "It has been a long time—"

Morgause frowned. "I found myself missing the Lake, and all those I love here," her daughter said then. "I did grow up here, after all."

"Indeed you did!" Ebrdila smiled happily and patted her hand.

I feel ill, thought Igierne, but she managed a smile as well. Whether she liked it or not, Morgause was born of the old blood. The Isle of Maidens was her heritage.

"Tonight the moon shines full, and we will honor her. It will be good to see you in the circle once more."

"Not the ritual on the hilltop, I hope—" said Morgause.

"But of course. The night will be clear," her mother replied.

Morgause grimaced. "I had hoped to see the Cauldron again. Artor bears the Sword, but the Hallow that remains on this isle is its equal in power. I am surprised you do not make more use of it!"

Igierne lifted one eyebrow. Was *that* why Morgause had come? "Would you take a war-axe to slice cheese? Neither Sword nor Cauldron are to be used unless need compels."

"True, but unless you practice with a weapon, you won't know how to use it when the need does arrive. Your son bears the Sword, but the Cauldron is my inheritance. Is it not time I began to learn its mysteries?"

From the look on her daughter's face, Igierne feared she had not been able to conceal her instinctive alarm.

"Not while you are still a mother and a ruling queen," she kept her voice even with an effort, wondering why she felt so reluctant to let her daughter anywhere near the Cauldron, since what Morgause had said was quite true. "I myself did not even begin to understand it until I was done with all that and retired to the Lake to give my whole heart to its Mysteries."

"No doubt you are right." Morgause shrugged dismissively. "And I am sure the ceremony on the heights will be very beautiful. It has been some time since I did much climbing, but if you can get up the mountain at your age, I should be able to manage as well."

"No doubt—" Igierne echoed with an edged smile. She had better walk by the lake this afternoon and meditate, she told herself, to clear her mind of anger before the ritual.

* * *

"Lady of the Silver Wheel,
Lady of the Three-fold Way,
Dreams and Destiny you deal,
Hear us, Goddess, as we pray . . ."

Women's voices echoed, soft and sweet across the water as the procession followed the path by the shore.

"Lady of the shining road,
Lady of the sacred round,
Holiness is your abode,
Help and healing there abound."

Breath shortened as the trail turned from the lake and began to wind up the hillside, but still the priestesses sang. Cupped by its encircling mountains, the island on the lake contained powerful magic, but by the time the full moon breasted those heights, it was high in the sky. The priestesses used the meadow where lay the circle of stones, where they could observe the moment she lifted above the horizon, to honor her.

Igierne felt the blood sing in her veins as the exercise warmed her, and smiled. Ebrdila no longer made this journey, but she herself could still keep up with the youngest of her priestesses. It was Morgause whose face was growing red with exertion as they climbed.

"Lady of the starry sky,
Lady of the sparkling sea,
Queen of all the hosts on high,
And the deeps of memory—"

They reached the summit at last, their shadows stretching black across the grass as the sun sank behind them. Northward, a cloudbank still hung in the heavens, but in the east the sky, tinted a pearly pink by sunset, was clear. Igierne could hear her daughter's harsh breathing ease as they spiraled around the slab of stone that lay on the grass. Cup and ring marks had been carved into its surface by some people long forgotten. Several still held a little water from the morning's rain.

"Lady of the moon's red tide,
Lady of the flowing breast,
Ever-changing, you abide,
Grant us motion, give us rest."

As each woman passed the stone, she bent, touched fingertip to the water and blessed herself, belly and breast and brow. Igierne felt her knee joints complain as she took her turn, and her sight darkened for a moment as she straightened again, but she kept her balance and moved on. She shook her head in self-mockery, knowing that if Morgause had not been there she would have stopped a moment to catch her breath at the top of the hill.

Eastward, the hills fell away in long folds to a dim haze that hid the more settled lands. And there, at the limit of vision, a luminous pallor was beginning to suffuse the sky. The priestesses waited, humming softly. The air brightened suddenly as the sun hung for an instant on the rim of the hills behind them. Then it was gone, and the world was lit by a gentle afterglow. Silently Igierne began to count, know-

ing that beyond the mountain the sun was still sinking towards the distant sea. The colors of the sky above deepened,
the clouds catching the light in bands of gold and rose. She
heard her own indrawn breath repeated around the semicir-
cle, and they began to sing once more.

> *"Radiant Lady, bless the night,*
> *Bless the waters and the skies,*
> *Bless the world with silver light,*
> *We summon you—arise, arise!"*

Every month they honored the full moon, on the Isle when
the weather was cloudy, and on the heights when the sky
was clear, yet the hair lifted on Igierne's neck as a growing
glow silhouetted the shape of a distant hill. And then, as if
in answer to the compulsion of the song's final line, they saw
the hill edged by a rim of blinding silver, and the huge, wonderful disc of the moon rose suddenly into the eastern sky.

Without thought she found her own arms rising with those
of the others, as if to lift that bright orb into the sky. Swiftly
the moon mounted the heavens, until the women stood with
arms stretched high in adoration, hailing the Goddess with a
wordless ululation of pure sound.

Gradually the human song faded until only the jubilant
chirring of crickets could be heard. Some of the priestesses
remained standing with uplifted arms to pray silently while
others sank to the earth, sitting cross-legged with their hands
open upon their knees. Igierne stayed where she was, staring
at the moon's brightness until vision was overwhelmed by
light.

Lady, hear and help me! her heart cried. *Here stands the child
of my body—why do I find it so hard to love her? She is my daughter, not my enemy!* She heard the harsh rasp of her breath and
stopped, willing the inner babble to still, remembering the
many times she had told young priestesses that it did no good
to ask the gods questions if you were not willing to listen for
the answer.

She could hear Morgause breathing beside her. After a

time, she realized they had found the same rhythm. She felt ashamed that she should be so surprised.

Is that Your answer? She stopped the thought, concentrating on her breathing, waiting. The moon was halfway up the sky, its color changing from the warm pearl glow of the horizon to a pure silver light. Listening, she heard Morgause's steady breathing grow ragged, as if she were trying to hold back tears.

What does she *have to cry about?* was Igierne's first, swiftly suppressed response. If this woman whose arrogance had irritated her so this afternoon was weeping, her sorrow must be all the greater for being hidden. There were those who must have thought the same of Igierne herself, in the days when she mourned secretly for her lost son while all men hailed her as Uthir's queen.

Ah, child, there was a time you would have brought your trouble to me and wept in my arms. How have we become such strangers? She turned to her daughter, intending to offer comfort. As she met Morgause's eyes, the younger woman's gaze grew stony and she turned away, but not before Igierne had seen upon her cheeks the silver track of tears.

Igierne stared at her back, feeling the tears start in her own eyes. *Sweet Lady, help her! Help us all!* came her heart's silent cry.

In the next moment a breath of wind stirred the grass and gently touched her hair. As it dried her cheeks, she thought that with it came a whisper, *"I am with you, even in your pain. . . ."*

As the harvest moon waned the north lay at peace. The grain was ripening, and on both sides of the Bodotria estuary, men labored to reap the golden sheaves. Braced against the side of the boat that was carrying her over the water, Morgause turned her face to the sea wind and breathed in freedom.

Leudonus was still in the south with Artor, and when Morgause announced her intention to visit the lady Tulach in Fodreu, there was no one in Dun Eidyn with the power to say her nay. Medraut had screamed when she detached his little hands from her gown and handed him to his nurse, but even his cries had no power against the imperative that ever since her visit to the Lake had beat like a drum in her brain—

My mother still loves Artor more! She will never share her secrets. Whatever magic I wield must be my own!

The land on the Pictish shore of the estuary was much the same as the country around Dun Eidyn. Why, she wondered, did the air seem fresher, and the colors more intense, on the other side? It was not only the change of scene that excited her, thought Morgause, for the Lake Country that surrounded the Isle of Maidens was a different land entirely, and she had only felt more constricted there. Perhaps it was because among the Picts she was bound by no ties of love or duty, only by whatever mutual obligations she should agree to in her search for power.

Tulach was waiting for her on the shore, accompanied by a half dozen tribesmen wrapped in tattered plaids and two older women in dusty black robes. They had enough ponies for the Votadini as well.

"Are you taking me to Fodreu?" asked Morgause as she mounted the shaggy little mare they had brought for her. Her own escort eyed the Pictish warriors uneasily, but with or without the consent of kinfolk, there had been marriages enough across the border that half of them had relations on the other side. As they moved out, their suspicions began to submerge in a murmur of genealogical comparison.

Tulach shook her head. "The place for the ritual I have in mind for you lies farther up the coast. We should reach it before nightfall."

"What is it?"

"A place of the old ones, who were here before Roman or Briton. The Picts are partly of that blood. You have such circles in the south as well, but you have forgotten how to use their magic. The old powers are still there, if you know how to call them. You will see."

Merlin knows how to call them, thought Morgause, remembering stories she had heard. Did she truly want to wield that magic, so ancient it seemed alien to her kind? But she had come too far to turn back now.

Her mother would never dream of challenging Merlin. Her mother, she reflected bitterly, was content to follow a woman's traditional path, supporting, encouraging, waiting in the shadows. Did Artor even bother to read the advice she sent him?

She took a deep breath of the damp sea-wind. Her older boys were already moving into Leudonus' world, but Medraut was still hers alone. *It is not advice I will give him, but commands*, she thought grimly, *when I come into my power. The princes of Britannia dream of bringing back the old days before they went under the yoke of Rome. I will bring back a time that is older still, the time of the queens!*

The rough-coated ponies made surprisingly swift progress on the uneven ground. By the afternoon they had travelled a fair distance north and eastward along the shore. They passed a village of fishermen, their overturned coracles sprouting like mushrooms from the stony strand, and paused for a meal of barley cakes baked on the hearthstone and washed down with heather beer. When they mounted once more, they took a new trail that wound upward through the shelving cliffs to a band of woodland below the moor. One of the warriors was now carrying a bag before him, with something inside it that jerked and struggled as they began to climb.

Just as dusk was falling they passed through a tangle of ash and alder where a small burn trickled towards the sea. Beyond it, an area roughly the size of Leudonus' hall had been roughly cleared. In the last of the light she could see that it was bordered by a circle of stones, the largest no more than waist-high. They were too choked by undergrowth to count, but the grass around the three in the center, one upright and the others tumbled, had been cut so that they stood clear.

As the priestesses dismounted, some of the warriors bound torches to the poles that had been set into the ground, and the bag was laid beside a tree. Then the men saluted Tulach and led the ponies back down the hill.

"They know better than to be near when women work magic!" the Pictish woman laughed. From her bag she took two black mantles, one of which she handed to Morgause.

"Take off your clothes and put this on. Then wait here until we call."

True, the wind was growing cold, but Morgause suspected it was the touch of the garment itself that had set her to shivering. To change one's semblance was to change the soul; as the black wool replaced the garments of the queen of the Votadini, she became someone else, someone she did not know.

The other women had already lit the torches and suspended a bronze kettle above a fire. The water inside it was beginning to steam. Morgause felt her lips twist in bitter amusement—it appeared that she was going to learn the mysteries of the cauldron after all.

Tulach moved sunwise around the inside of the circle, scattering herbs and chanting something in the old tongue. Morgause blinked, wondering if it were the gathering dusk that suddenly made it so hard to see.

Through the gloom she glimpsed Tulach coming towards her.

"Who are you, and why have you come here?"

"I am Morgause daughter of Igierne," she heard herself answering, "and I come to offer my service to the old powers."

"That is well. Take up the offering—" she indicated the bag "—and enter."

What happened after that was hard to remember. There was more chanting in the strange language as the three old women cast herbs and mushrooms and other nameless things into the cauldron. The aromatic steam made Morgause dizzy, so that sometimes she thought she saw a host of shapes around them and at others it was only the three.

"We stand upon the graves of old ones," Tulach told her. "Do not be surprised if they are drawn to the ceremony."

Shortly thereafter the singing reached a climax. It was full dark now; in the circle the flickering torches chased shadows around the fire.

"Take up the bag," said Tulach, "and carefully bring out what you find there."

Morgause had already concluded it must be an animal, and was not surprised to find she had hold of a large hare. Everyone knew that the hare was a creature of great magic. A fisherman who saw one on his way to the boats would turn back and stay home that day. It was never hunted, never eaten except when it was offered to the Goddess. At first the beast struggled, but when she made it breathe the steam, it abruptly went still. Tulach grasped it by the ears and handed her a flint knife.

"Kill it—" she said, "and give the blood to the stones."

The stone knife was sharper than she had expected, but it was still a messy business. Then Morgause got the big vein open, and held the body so that blood spurted over the rock, pooling in the hollows and running down the sides. One of the other women took the victim and began to skin it, and in a few minutes the disjointed body was simmering in the cauldron with the herbs.

The head sat dripping on the largest stone, and Morgause blinked, for the rock was surrounded by a pale glow. She looked around her and saw that the other stones were glowing as well with a light that owed nothing to the fire. With every movement, Tulach and the three priestesses trailed a glimmering radiance. Morgause felt her head swim and knew that she was already deep in trance. The tiny spark within that could still think yammered frantically. Why should they stop with the hare, when they could sacrifice a Votadini queen?

The other women had stripped off their black robes. For a moment she thought that beneath they were wearing blue-embroidered garments. Then she realized that she was seeing skin, tattooed in intricate patterns with woad. She was too dazed to prevent them from removing her black mantle as well, but within the circle the air was warm.

Tulach began to speak, her voice blurred as if it came through water. "We will make no permanent mark upon your skin, but the sacred signs we paint upon your body will mark your spirit shape so that the powers can see . . ."

She dipped a small brush into a bowl in which hare's blood had been mixed with something else and began to draw upon Morgause's breast and belly the same spirals that marked her own. The brush tickled as it passed, and left a tingling behind it. By the time the priestesses had finished painting her front and back, upper arms and thighs, her entire body was throbbing with a pleasant, almost sexual pain.

The soft heartbeat of a drum brought Morgause to her feet again.

"Now you are ready . . . now we call *Her*. . . ."

The drum beat faster, and Morgause found herself dancing as she had not danced since before her first child. Sweat sheened her body, adding its own meanders to the painted designs; she could smell her own female musk mingling with the scent of the herbs. It was very late; the distorted husk of the waning moon hung in the eastern sky.

The priestesses were singing. Presently Morgause recognized goddess-names within the murmur of incantation. She began to listen more carefully, understanding without knowing whether she was hearing with the ears or the heart.

The goddesses they were calling were older and wilder than any face of the Lady she had heard of on the Isle, names that resonated in earth and fire, in the stone of the circle and the whisper of the distant sea.

"Call Her!" sang Tulach as she whirled by. "Call Her by the name of your deepest desire!"

For a moment Morgause faltered. Then the drumming drew from her belly a moan, a shout, a cry of rage she had not known she held within.

She spun in place, light and shadow whirling around her. And then it was not shadow, but ravens, a cloud of black birds whose hoarse cries echoed her own.

"Cathubodva! Cathubodva! Come!"

Was she still moving, or was it the birds who swept her up to the heart of the maelstrom, where it was suddenly, shockingly, still?

"You have called Me, and I have come . . . what do you need?"

"I want what my mother had, what my brother has! I have as much right as he does to rule—I want to be Tigernissa—I want to be queen!"

"The power of the Black Raven, not the White, is Mine. I am the Dark Face of the Moon . . ." came the answer. *"I madden the*

complacent and destroy that which is outworn. I drink red blood and feast upon the slain...."

"My mother clings to a power she can no longer wield! My brother fights for a dream that died with Rome! Let me be your priestess, Lady, and do your will!"

"*What will you sacrifice?*"

"I have a young son, who is also the son of the king! Help me, and I will raise him to be your champion!"

Abruptly sound returned in a cacophony that whirled her with it into a chaos of fire and shadow until she knew no more.

FIRST BLOOD

A.D. 494

Bushes blurred by in a haze of green as Guendivar beat her heels against the white pony's sides. Then they burst out onto the sunny ridge, and the mare, seeing a clear trail before her, stretched out her neck and responded with a new burst of speed. Guendivar tightened her long legs around the blanket and whooped in delight. She was flying, lifting like a bird into the blue.

Then the road dipped, and the pony began to slow. Guendivar dug in her heels, but the mare snorted, shaking her head, and her canter became a jarring trot that compelled the girl to rein her in.

"Oh, very well—" she said crossly. "I suppose you deserve a rest. But you liked it too, didn't you, my swan? I wish you could really fly!"

Guendivar had gotten the pony for her seventh birthday. Now she was thirteen; too old, said her mother, to spend her days careering about the countryside. The dark shadow of adulthood was creeping towards her. Only on Cygnet's back could she be free.

A gull's cry brought her head up; she followed its flight, shading her eyes against the sunlight, as it wheeled above the

ridge and away over the Vale. It had been a beautiful summer, especially after last year, when there was so much rain.
Through the mist she glimpsed the distant glitter of the Sabrina estuary. Closer, golden haze lay across the lowlands,
reminding her of the waters that in the winter turned it into
an inland sea. A few hillocks poked through like islands,
dominated by a pointed cone in the middle of the Vale. In
this light, even the Tor seemed luminous; she wondered if
that was why some folk called it the Isle of Glass.

The pony had halted and was tugging at the rein as she
tried to reach the grass. Guendivar hauled the beast's head
up and got her going again, frowning as she became aware
of a dull ache across her lower back. In a canter, Cygnet was
as graceful as the bird from which she took her name, but her
trot was torture.

Suddenly the bag of apples and bread and cheese tied to
her belt seemed very attractive. Guendivar gave the pony a
kick and reined her down the hill towards the spring.

It was little more than a seep in the side of the hill, but the
constant trickle of water had hollowed out a small pool,
fringed with fern and stone-crop and shaded by a willow tree.
On the sunny slopes, the grass was ripening, but near the
spring the spreading moisture had kept it a vivid green. Cygnet tugged at the rein, eager to be at it, and laughing, Guendivar swung her right foot over the pony's neck and slid
down.

"You are a goose, not a swan," she exclaimed, "and just as
greedy. But while we eat we may as well be comfortable."
She turned to uncinch the blanket and stilled, staring at the
blood that had soaked into the cloth.

Frantically she unbuckled the cinch and pulled off the blanket, searching for the injury. But the pony's sweat-darkened
hide was whole.

Guendivar's racing pulse thundered in her ears. She teth-
ered the mare so that she could graze, and then, very reluc-
tantly, she loosened her breeches, a pair that had been her
older brother's when he was a boy, and pulling them down,
saw on the inseam the betraying red stain.

Swearing softly, she pulled the breeches off. She could

wash them, and no one would know. But even as she bent over the pool she felt warmth, and saw a new trickle of red snake down her inner thigh.

That was when panic changed to despair, and she curled up on the grass and let the hot tears flow.

Guendivar was still sniffling when she became aware that she was not alone. In that first moment, she could not have told what had changed. It was like hearing music, though there was no sound, or a scent, though there was no change in the air. As she sat up, her senses settled on vision as a mode of perception, and she saw a shimmer that she recognized as the spirit of the pool. Words formed in her awareness.

"You are different today . . ."

"I've got my moonblood," Guendivar said bitterly, "and now everything is going to change!"

"Everything is always changing. . . ."

"Some changes are worse than others. Now my mother will make me stay home and spin while she talks to me about ruling a house and a husband! After this, she'll never let me ride alone again! I don't want this blood! I don't want to change!"

"It was the blood that called me," came the reply.

"What?" She opened her eyes again. "I thought growing up would mean I couldn't see you."

"Not so. When you are in your blood it will be easier. . . ."

Guendivar felt the hairs lift on her arms. Around her the air was thickening with glimmering forms: the slender shape of the Willow girl bending over her; spirits of reed and flower; airy forms that drifted on the wind; squat shapes that emerged from the stones.

"Why are you here?" she whispered. "What does my woman blood mean to you?"

"It means life. It means you are part of the magic."

"I thought it just meant having babies. I don't want to be worn out like my mother, bearing child after child that dies." Petronilla had borne eight infants, but only the oldest boys and Guendivar survived.

"When man and maid lie down together in the fields they make

magic. Before, you were only a bud on the branch. Now you are the flower."

Guendivar sat back, thinking about that. Abruptly she found herself hungry. She reached for the bag, and then, remembering, started to offer a portion to the pool.

"You have something better to give us—" came the voices around her. *"There is a special power in the first spurting of a boy's seed, and a girl's first flow. Wash yourself in the spring. . . ."*

Guendivar flushed with embarrassment, even though she knew that human conventions meant less than nothing to the faerie kind. But gradually her shame shifted to something else, a dawning awareness of power. She bent, and scooping up the cool water in her palm, poured it over her thighs until her blood swirled dark in the clear water. When she was clean, she washed out her breeches and the saddle cloth and laid them out in the sun to dry.

The faerie folk flitted around her in swirls of light.

"Sleep a little . . . " said the spirit of the pool, *"and we will send you dreams of power."*

Guendivar lay back and closed her eyes. Almost immediately images began to come: the running of the deer, mare and stallion, sow and boar, men and women circling the Beltain fire. All the great dance of life whirled before her, faster and faster, shaping itself at last into the figure of a laughing maiden formed out of flowers.

When she woke at last, the setting sun had turned all the vale into a blaze of gold. But the spirits had disappeared. Her clothing was dry, and for the moment, her flow of blood seemed to have ceased. Swiftly she dressed and cinched the saddle cloth back onto the mare. She was still not looking forward to telling her mother what had happened. But one thing had changed—the thought of growing up no longer made her afraid.

For all the years of Guendivar's childhood, the Tor had been a constant presence, felt, even when clouds kept it from being seen. But except for one visit made when she was too little to remember, she had never been there. As soon as she told her mother what had happened to her, Petronilla had decided to take her to the nuns who lived on the Isle of Glass for a blessing. The prospect filled her with mingled excitement and fear.

It is like growing up— she thought as they reached the base of the isle and the curve of the lower hill hid the Tor from view. *For so long it loomed on the horizon, and now I cannot see it because I am almost there. I will only be able to see my own womanhood reflected in others' eyes.*

The top of the round church that the holy Joseph had built showed above the trees. Around it clustered the smaller huts that were the monks' cells, and a little farther, a second group of buildings for the nuns. Nearby was the guesthouse where the visitors would stay. As they climbed the road, the deep sound of men's voices throbbed in the air. The monks were chanting the noon prayers, her mother said. Guendivar felt the hair lift on her arms with delight as the sweet sounds drifted through the trees. Then the shadowed orifice of the church door came into view and she shivered. The music was beautiful, but cooped up in the darkness like that, how could men sing?

She sighed with relief as they continued along the hillside toward the houses of the nuns. To one side she saw apple trees, ripening fruit already weighting their branches, and to the other, neat gardens. Beyond was a tall hedge, hiding the base of the hill that nestled next to the Tor. She wondered what was behind it. There was something in the air of this place that made her skin tingle as it did when the faerie folk were near. If she could escape her mother's watchful eye, this would be a good place to explore.

A tall woman came out of one of the houses, robed in a shapeless gown of natural wool with a wooden cross hanging from a thong around her neck, her hair hidden by a linen veil. But when she looked up, Guendivar saw a broad smile and twinkling eyes. For a moment that gaze rested on her in frank appraisal. Then she turned to Guendivar's mother.

"So, Petronilla, this is your maid-child—she has grown like a flower in good soil, tall and fair!"

"Nothing so rooted," answered her mother ruefully. "She

is a bird, or perhaps a wild pony, always off running about the hills. Guendivar, this is Mother Maruret. Show that you know how to give her a proper greeting!"

Still blushing, Guendivar slid down from her pony, took the woman's hand and bent to kiss it.

"You are welcome indeed, my child. My daughters will show you to your quarters. No doubt you will wish to wash before your meal."

Guendivar's belly growled in anicipation. Along with other changes, she was growing, and these days she was always hungry.

"You are not our only guests," said Mother Maruret as she led them towards the largest building. "The queen is here."

"Igierne?" asked Petronilla.

"Herself, with two of her women."

Petronilla lifted one eyebrow. "And you allow them to stay on the Isle?"

The nun smiled. "We have been in this place long enough to understand that the ways of the Creator of the World are many and mysterious. If the queen is deluded, how shall that trouble my own faith? But indeed, she has never been other than quiet and respectful when she was here . . ."

Guendivar listened, wide-eyed. She had heard many tales of Artor's mother, the most beautiful woman of her time. They said that King Uthir had fought a war to win her and killed her husband before her eyes, though others whispered that Merlin had murdered him with his magic. She lived now in the north, ran the tales, on a magic island. Of course by now Igierne must be quite old, but it would be exciting to meet her all the same.

But when they entered the guest-house, though the queen's two women were there, talking softly by the fire, Igierne was nowhere to be seen.

Just before dawn, Guendivar's mother awakened her. The girl rose quickly and dressed in the white gown they gave her—she had been fasting since noon the day before before, and the sooner this was over the sooner she could get some food. Stumbling with sleepiness, she followed her mother and the two nuns, one of them young and one an old woman, who led the way with lanterns out of the guesthouse and up the hill.

Her interest quickened when she saw they were approaching the hazel hedge. There was a gate set amid the branches. The young woman lifted the iron latch and motioned for them to go in.

On the other side was a garden. Already a few birds were singing, though the sky was still dim and grey. She could hear the tinkle of falling water, and as the light grew, she saw that it was flowing down through a stone channel into a large pool.

"The spring is farther up the hill," the young nun said in a low voice. Her name, she remembered, was Julia. "Winter and summer the pure water flows from the holy well. Even in years of drought it has never failed."

Petronilla glanced at the sky, then turned to her daughter. "It is almost time. Take off the gown and step into the pool."

"I was baptized when I was a babe," muttered Guendivar as she obeyed, "Was not that not purification enough?"

"This is to cleanse you from childhood's sins. You will emerge, a woman, transformed by the blood of your body and the water of the spirit." Her mother took the gown and folded it across her arm.

Of the spirit, or the spirits? wondered Guendivar, remembering the spring on the hillside. It gave her the courage to set her foot on the steps that entered the dark water.

In that first shocked moment, she could not tell if the water was holy, only that it was freezingly cold. She stifled a yelp and stood shaking, the water lapping the joining of her thighs.

"In the name of the Blessed Virgin, may you be cleansed and purified of all sin and stain..." murmured Sister Julia, dipping up water in a wooden bowl and pouring it over Guendivar's shoulders.

"In the name of Maria Theotokos, may you be cleansed and purified—" Now it was her mother's turn.

"In the name of the Lady of Sorrows..." The old nun poured water over her head and stepped away.

In the name of all the gods, let me out of here before I freeze!

thought Guendivar, edging back towards the steps. But her mother stopped her with a word. When Guendivar could escape her mother's eye, she ran free, but she had never yet dared to defy her directly. Shivering, the girl stood where she was.

The sky brightened to a luminous pink like the inside of a shell. Light lay like a mist above the water. Guendivar took a quick breath, and realized that her shivering had ceased and her skin was tingling.

"Spirit of the holy spring," her lips moved silently, "give me your blessing . . ." She scooped up water in her hand and drank, surprised at its iron tang. Then, before she could lose courage, she took a quick breath and submerged herself in the pool.

For a long moment she stayed there, her amber hair raying out across the surface, and each hair on her body lifted by its own bubble of air. The water she had swallowed sent a shock through every vein. The tingling of her skin intensified, as if the water were penetrating all the way to her bones. Then, just as it reached the edge of pain, it became light. The force of it brought Guendivar upright, arms uplifted, turning to face the rising sun.

She heard a sharp gasp of indrawn breath from one of the women. The sun was rising red above the slope of the hill. Rosy light glistened on her wet skin, glittered from the surface of the pool. For a moment she gazed, then the light brightened to gold and she could look no more.

"Receive the blessing of the Son of God—" her mother cried. But it was another voice that Guendivar heard.

"Be blessed by the shining sun, for while you walk in its light, no other power shall separate you from this bright and living world. . . ."

To that dawn ritual there was one other witness, who watched from the hillside as the women helped Guendivar from the pool and hid the radiance of her body in the shapeless robe of a penitent. When Igierne had first heard of the planned ritual, she had feared they meant to make the girl a nun; the actual intention was almost as hard to understand.

What sins could a child of thirteen have committed? Before her marriage, Petronilla had spent some time as part of Igierne's court. She came from an old Roman family that had long been Christian. Igierne knew that it was not the stains of childhood that Guendivar's mother wanted to wash away, but her daughter's incipient sexuality.

If so, she had chosen the wrong place to do so. Igierne knew how to interpret the blaze of light she had seen in the pool, and she knew also that the colony of monks established here by Joseph of Arimathea had learned how to use the magic of the Tor, but had not changed it. The powers that dwelt here were ancient when the Druids first saw this hill. She should not be surprised that this girl, whose face she had first seen in vision, should be recognized by the spirits of the Tor.

But it did make it all the more imperative that she speak with Guendivar. It would be difficult, for Petronilla kept her daughter well guarded. When the women had left the pool Igierne made her own way down to it, and found tangled in the branches above the gateway a wisp of red-gold hair. She smiled, and pulling a few pale hairs from her own head, began to twine them together, whispering a spell.

The little community on the Tor retired early, the guests to sleep through the night, and the nuns to rest until they should be called to midnight prayer. At night, said the Christians, the Devil roamed the world, and only the incantations of the faithful kept him at bay. But to Igierne, the night was a friend.

When the sound of quiet breathing told her that the other women in the guesthouse were asleep, she rose, slipped her feet into sandals and took up a cloak, and went outside. If anyone had questioned her, she would have said she sought the privy, but in fact her goal was the orchard, where she found a seat, put on the ring of twined hair she had made that morning, and began to sing.

And presently, just as the moon was lifting above the trees, the door to the guest-house opened and a pale figure came through. Igierne told herself that it was only the effect of moonlight on a white gown that made Guendivar's figure seem luminous, but she could not help remembering the radiance of the morning and wondering.

Still, this opportunity must not be wasted. As Guendivar started down the path, Igierne gathered up her cloak and came out to meet her.

The girl started, eyes widening, but she stood her ground.

"Couldn't you sleep either?" Igierne asked softly. "Let us walk. The gardens are beautiful in the light of the moon."

"You're human—" It was not quite a question.

"As human as you are," Igierne answered, although when she remembered what she had seen that morning, she wondered.

"You are the queen—" Guendivar said then.

"The queen that was," Igierne replied, *as you are the queen that will be. . . .* But it was not yet time to say so aloud.

They came out from beneath the moon-dappled shadows of the orchard and continued along the path. The moon shone full in a luminous sky, so bright that one could distinguish the red of the roses that lined the path from the dim green of the hill.

"Where are we going?" Guendivar asked at last.

"To the White Spring. You bathed in the Red Spring this morning, did you not? The Blood Well? Perhaps you did not know there is another on the Tor."

"The Blood Well?" the girl echoed. "Then that is why . . . I thought—" Her voice became a whisper. "I thought that my flow had started again, that my blood had turned the water red."

"They should have explained," Igierne said tartly. "There is iron in the water, just as there is in our blood. Did they tell you the water would wash away your sins? In the old days, maidens bathed here to establish their female cycle. Barren women came also, that their wombs might become as bountiful as the well."

"I felt a tingling . . . all through my body . . ." Guendivar said then. "I suppose that now my mother will be trying to marry me off. She is very ambitious. But I'm not ready."

"Indeed—" Igierne knew too well what it was to be married young to an older man. But for the daughters of princes, a long maidenhood was a luxury. And how long could Artor wait before his ministers compelled him to take a bride? "Do you think you will be ready when you are fifteen?"

The girl shrugged. "That is the age at which my brother was allowed to ride to battle."

"It is the age at which my son became king . . ."

"That was a long time ago," said Guendivar.

Igierne's heart sank. What were the gods about, to make Artor wait so many years for his destined bride? Silent, she led the way down the path to the second gate, and the smaller enclosure where the White Spring welled up from the ground.

"What is this one for?" the girl asked.

"They say it brings hope and healing. You are in health, but sometimes the spirit needs healing as well. Let the water flow into this bowl, and then hold it up to catch the light of the moon."

Guendivar nodded. "There was sun-power in the Blood Well, but this feels different—" She lifted the bowl.

"I wish—" Igierne began, then paused. The girl looked at her expectantly. "Not many would have noticed that. If I thought there were any chance your mother would agree, I would take you for training on the Holy Isle . . ." *If only I could give Artor a queen who was an initiate of the ancient mysteries!*

"An island?" Guendivar shook her head. "I would feel prisoned if I could not gallop my pony beneath the sky. Why do you you live there?"

"Long ago the Romans sought to destroy all Druids because they were the ones who preserved the soul of our people and reminded them of what it was to be free. Those who survived their attacks fled to Alba or Eriu, or secret places in Britannia where they could survive. The Lake is one such, hidden among high hills, and also it is very beautiful."

"I suppose—" the girl said dubiously. "But what do you find to do there all day?"

Igierne laughed. "Our life on the Isle of Maidens is not so different from the way the nuns live here, although we call ourselves maiden not because we are virgin but because we are bound to no man. We spin and weave and grow herbs as other women do, and beyond that, we pray. Do you think that sounds boring?" she answered Guendivar's grimace. "Our prayers are no abject plea to a distant god, but an act of magic. We seek to put ourselves in harmony with the flow of energy through the world, and by understanding, to bend it—"

"To change things?" Guendivar asked.

"To help them to become what they should be, that all shall prosper."

For a few moments Guendivar considered this, her hair glistening in the light of the moon. Then, very softly, came another question. "Do you talk to the spirits, the faerie-folk?"

"Sometimes . . ." answered Igierne.

"I see them . . . they are my best friends. . . ."

The touch of faerie! That is the source of the strangeness I have seen in her, thought Igierne.

The girl shrugged ruefully. "Now you know more than I have ever told my mother. Do not tell her that we have spoken. She already looks at you as if she feared you might summon a chariot drawn by dragons to carry me away!" She stopped abruptly, and even in the gloom Igierne could tell that she was blushing.

"Does she think the Tigernissa of Britannia without honor? You are still a child, and in her ward. I will say only this, Guendivar—if in time to come you need help or counsel, write to me."

She could love this girl, she thought then, as her own daughter—more, she feared, than she had ever been able to love Morgause. But when the child was married to Artor she *would* be her daughter. Surely the goddess who had sent her that vision would not lie!

Guendivar nodded, set the bowl to her lips, and drank. After a moment she lifted her head, her eyes wide with wonder.

"The moon is in it—" With a ceremonial grace, she offered the bowl.

Moonlight flashed silver from trembling water as Igierne grasped the rim. The water was very cold, so pure it tasted sweet on the tongue. She closed her eyes, and let that sweetness spread through her. *Grant hope and healing* . . . she prayed, *to me and to Britannia*. . . .

Igierne held onto the wooden seat as her cart bumped up the street towards the Governor's Palace. She had forgotten how hot Londinium could get in the days between Midsummer and Harvest. Heat radiated from the stone walls of those buildings that remained, and the trees that had grown up among the ruins of others drooped with dusty leaves. Ceincair and Morut swayed in stoic silence beside her.

She ached in every joint from the jolting of the cart, her tunic was stuck to her back with perspiration, and her hair was full of dust despite the veil. For a moment of piercing regret, she wished she had never left the Lake. But there were baths at the palace—perhaps she would feel better when she was clean.

And then the cart pulled up at the gates. Guards straightened to attention, calling out her name. One or two were men she remembered from her days with Uthir. She smiled, giving orders, and for a little while, forgot that she was not still the queen.

By the time the three priestesses were settled it was evening, and Artor had returned to the palace. That was a relief. When Igierne had stopped in Isca on the way south she had heard he was in Londinium, but at any moment that could change. These days he seemed to conduct the business of Britannia from the back of a horse. She had sent a message to warn him of her coming, but she would not have been surprised to find him gone.

He was obviously not intending to stay long. The palace was understaffed, and the meal to which they sat down, though well-cooked, was little better than camp fare.

"I don't know why I should be surprised," said Igierne, taking another spoonful of lentil stew. "When I married him, your father was living on the same thing."

Artor gave her a wry smile. "A telling argument for any who still doubt my parentage. But in truth, I eat this way for the same reason he did. We are still at war. Icel is holding to the treaty I forced on him last summer, but the Irish in De-

metia are making trouble again. I must ask you and your
ladies to continue your prayers for us, for I will have to take
my army westward soon."

Igierne sighed. Artor was taller, with a look that reminded
her of her mother about the eyes, but his hair was the same
nut brown, and his shoulders as broad as Uthir's had been.
As Artor grew older, the resemblance sometimes took her
breath away. Like Uthir, he was, in public, a Christian. But
he knew very well that the priestesses of the Isle of Maidens
did more than simply pray. That was not the issue now.

"No one who knew him would doubt that you are Uthir's
son. Nor do I dispute that Britannia is still at war. But during
all the years of our marriage it was the same. Nonetheless,
your father and I managed to live like civilized people. There
is no reason you cannot do so as well!"

"But I am not married . . ." he said softly, reaching for the
wine.

Igierne stared unseeing at the faded frescoes on the wall
behind him, thinking furiously. Every other time she had
brought up the subject, he had turned the conversation. Why
was he mentioning it now?

"Are you thinking of changing that?" she asked carefully.

Artor looked up, saw her face, and laughed. "Are you
afraid I've fallen in love with someone unsuitable? When
would I find the time?" He shook his head. "But even old
Oesc has managed to find a woman—Prince Gorangonus'
granddaughter, of all people. I've just returned from their
wedding, where I gave the bride away. I always meant to
marry once the country was secure, but at this rate, Oesc will
have grandchildren by then." He took a deep breath. "I'm
ready to consider it, mother, though I warn you, I have no
time to go looking for a bride."

Igierne sipped wine, for a moment too astounded by this
capitulation for words. "Perhaps you won't have to," she said
slowly. "If my visions have not lied. There is a maiden, Prince
Leodegranus' daughter, whom I believe the Goddess has chosen. But you will have to wait for her—she is only thirteen."

"She is a child!" he exclaimed.

"Any girl who is still unspoken for is going be young—"

said Igierne. "Unless you choose a widow, but that is likely to cause complications." They both heard the unspoken, *As it did for me . . .*

"I won't force a maid into marriage with a man twice her age," Artor said grimly. "We must meet before things are settled."

"I will write to Leodegranus, and ask him not to betroth his daughter until you have seen her."

"She must be willing."

"Of course . . ." said Igierne, sighing. She herself had been willing to marry Gorlosius, and that had been a disaster. "Your sister had doubts about marrying Leudonus," she said aloud, "but she agreed to do it, and that pairing seems to have worked out well, even though he is much older than she."

She tried to interpret the play of expression on Artor's face at the mention of Morgause. She knew her daughter resented *him*, but Artor had hardly met his sister often enough to form an opinion.

"I have not seen her since we defeated Naiton Morbet and the Picts," he said finally. "She was . . . magnificent. Three of her boys are with me now, and they tell me that she is well."

Igierne nodded. "I last saw her five years ago, when she visited the Lake with her youngest child. She seemed troubled, but Leudonus was not the cause."

"What, then?" Artor straightened, and she knew he was thinking like a king once more.

"Since Medraut, there have been no more children, and Morgause is a woman who cherished her fertility. She wanted me to make her priestess of the Cauldron—I suspect she was looking for a new source of power."

"I knew you had kept the Sword of the Defender on the Isle of Maidens, but what is the Cauldron?" Artor asked.

"Perhaps, if there is ever a season of peace, you can visit the Lake and I will show you. It is a woman's mystery, but you are the High King, and there are some things you have a right to know." She paused, marshalling her memories. "It is silver . . . very ancient." She shook her head. "That is only what it looks like, not what it *is*. . . . The Cauldron . . . is the womb of the Goddess, the vessel from which comes the power to renew the world."

For a long moment, Artor simply stared. Then she saw a new light come into his eyes. ". . . To renew the world," he echoed. "Do you know how I have dreamed of it? I have been High King of Britannia since I was fifteen years old, and spent most of that time defending her. Do you understand what that means, Mother? All I have been able to do is react, to try and maintain the status quo. How I have longed to move forward, to make things better, to heal this land! If there is ever, as you say, a season of peace, I will beg you to invoke the Cauldron's power!"

Igierne reached out, and Artor took her hand. Her heartbeat was shaking her chest. For so long she had loved her son, yearned for him, and never known him at all. And now it seemed to her that she touched his soul through their clasped hands.

"I will be ready, my beloved. Together we will do it. This is what I too have been waiting for, all my life long!"

But even as her heart soared in triumph, Igierne wondered how Morgause was likely to react when she learned that Artor had been given yet one more thing that she herself had been denied.

Medraut was telling a story. Morgause heard his voice as she came around the side of the women's sun house, clear as a bard's, rising and falling as he spun out the tale.

"It was old Nessa's spirit I saw . . . hunched beside the fire just as when she lived. And anyone who takes that seat is her prey—first you'll feel a cold touch on your neck, and then—"

From the corner of his eye he saw his mother coming and fell silent. The younger children to whom he had been talking got to their feet, wide-eyed at the sight of the queen.

"Medraut, you will follow me—"

"As you wish, Mama," he answered politely. She had taught him not to talk back to her before he was three years old.

But as they neared the door she heard a stifled giggle from one of the children, and turning, surprised her son completing a swish of his hips that was obviously an imitation of her own walk. Her hand shot out and she gripped his ear and hauled him after her through the door.

"And what was *that?*" she asked, releasing him.

"Nothing—it was just to make them laugh," he added as she reached for him again, "so they'll like me."

Her fingers clenched in his hair, jerking it for emphasis. "You are a *prince*, Medraut. It is they who should be courting *you!* But if you *must* ridicule, attack those who are lower than yourself. It does not contribute to *your* standing to make them laugh at *me!* Do you understand?"

"I understand, Mama . . ." he whispered, and she let him go. His eyes glittered with tears, but weeping was another thing she had trained him out of long ago.

"You are a prince, my beloved," Morgause added, more gently. She set down the bag she was carrying, and bent, turning him to face her and gently stroking his hair. "Your blood is the highest in the land. And you are the brightest and best of my children. Remember that, Medraut. I will teach you things that none of the others could understand. You must not disappoint me, my little one. . . ." She took his face between her hands and kissed him on the brow.

As she straightened, she saw his gaze shift to the bag, which was twitching and bulging of its own accord.

"Is it alive?" he whispered.

"That is a surprise for you," she answered gaily, picking up the bag with one hand and offering the other to her son. As always, her heart lifted as his small fingers tightened on hers. *You are mine!* she thought, looking down at him, *the child of my heart and the son of my soul!*

"Are we going to do a ritual?" he asked as the turned down the path to the spring. "Is it something that you have been learning from Tulach and her friends?"

"Hush, child, we must not speak of that here," said Morgause. "What we will do is not one of their rites, though they have helped me to better understand it. You are seven years old. What I will show you today will set you on the road to power."

Medraut began to walk faster, and she smiled.

By the time they reached the spring, the sun was setting at the end of the gorge, and as it disappeared, the shadow of the cliff loomed dark across the grass. Sounds from the dun above them came to them faintly, as though from another world.

Morgause dropped the bag and hunkered down beside it, motioning to Medraut to do the same.

"This is the hour that lies between day and night. Now, we are between times, between the worlds. It is a good time to speak with spirits, and those that dwell in the sacred springs and holy wells are among the most powerful."

He nodded, gazing into the dark pool with wondering eyes. What did he see? When Morgause was a child she had sometimes glimpsed the faerie-folk. These days, she was learning to do so again, with the aid of certain herbs and spells.

Carefully, she showed him how to cleanse head and hands, and made him drink a little from the spring.

"Make your prayer to the spirit that lives here . . ."

Obediently he shut his eyes, lips moving silently. She would rather have heard what he was saying, but that did not matter now. Presently he looked up at her once more.

In the distance Morgause could hear the lowing of cattle, but by the spring it was very still. But there was a weight to that silence, as if something was listening. She picked up the bag and smiled.

"The spirit of the spring is waiting. Now you must make your offering. Open the bag—"

With nimble fingers, Medraut untied the strings and pulled at the opening, dropping it with a squawk as something white and feathered burst free. It was a cockerel, and it was not happy at having been confined in the bag. But its feet had been tied, so for all its flapping, it could not go far.

"Blood is life," said Morgause. "Wring the bird's neck, and let its blood flow into the pool."

Medraut looked from the cockerel to his mother and shook his head, eyes dark with revulsion.

"What, are you afraid of a little blood? When you are a warrior, you will have to kill men! Do it, Medraut—do it now!"

The child shook his head again and started to edge away. Morgause fought to control her anger.

"I teach you secrets that grown men would pay to learn. You will not deny me. See—" she gentled her voice, "it is easy—"

With a swift pounce, she captured his hands and pressed them around the neck of the fowl. The boy fought to free himself, still shaking his head and weeping. Morgause could not afford pity. Tightening her grip, she twisted, ripped the cockerel's head off and tossed it aside. Medraut cried out as blood spurted, but still she held his hands on the body of the bird, and did not know if the tremors that pulsed through their clasped fingers were those of the dying cockerel or of her son.

LADY OF THE EASTERN GATE

A.D. 495

In the hour before dawn, the priestesses gathered in the largest of the roundhouses on the Isle of Maidens. Mist lay like a veil across the lake; glittered in golden haloes around the lamps. Silent and anxious, some still rubbing sleep from their eyes, they filed in and took their places around the hearth.

Igierne was waiting for them. From sunset of the night before, when her spirit, open in the evening meditation, had received Merlin's message to this moment, she had not been able to sleep at all. Since the beginning of this last and greatest Saxon rebellion, the priestesses had met three times daily to support with the strength of their spirits the Britons' campaign.

But this was the last battle, the final confrontation with the ancient enemy. Through Merlin's eyes she had seen the hill called Mons Badonicus where Artor's army stood at bay, the scattering of campfires on its summit surrounded by a multitude below. The men were tired, food was low, and their water was almost gone. With the dawning, they would stake all on one last throw and ride against the enemy.

The priestesses, huddled in their pale mantles against the

chill, sat like a circle of stones, and like the stones, their strength was rooted in the earth of Britannia. With Igierne, they were nineteen—all the senior priestesses, and the most talented of the girls. She signaled to the drummer to begin her steady beat. Then she took a deep breath and let her own awareness sink down through the fluid layers around the island and deeper still into the bedrock that supported them. Slowly her pulsebeat steadied and her breathing slowed. Here, at the foundation of all things, there was neither hope nor fear. There was only pure Being, changeless and secure.

She could have remained in that safe and secret place forever, but though her anxiety had faded, the discipline of years brought her back to awareness of her need, fueled by her determination and deeper even than her fear for her country, to protect her child. Slowly she allowed her awareness to move upward, trailing a cord of connection to the earth below, until she reached the level where her body sat once more.

Igierne lifted her arms, and the drumming quickened. With the precision of long practice, the other priestesses stretched out their arms. One by one they connected, and as the circle was completed, a pulse of power flared from hand to hand. Now, with each breath, power was drawn up from the depths and through the body, out through the left palm to the hand it clasped and onward.

Around and around, with each circuit it grew, a vortex that spiraled above the hearth. Igierne kept it steady, resisting the temptation to release it all in one climactic explosion of energy. In her mind she held the image of Merlin, offering him the cone of power to support his own wizardry. As the link grew stronger, she sensed men and horses, confusion and blood-lust, exaltation and fear.

She held the circle even as she felt something flare towards him like a spear of light. But the shock as Merlin caught it shattered the link. For one terrified moment the spirits of the priestesses were tossed like leaves in a high wind. And then another power blossomed in the midst of them, rising from the hearth like a flame into which all other powers were subsumed.

Bright as fire, serene as pure water, strong as the earth below, Brigantia Herself arose from the midst of Her priestesses and directed their joined powers towards the goddess image on the boss of Artor's shield. Through Her eyes, Igierne saw the image blaze, saw an answering radiance in the faces of Britannia's warriors, and saw, as the Saxons felt the land itself turning against them, the enemy break and flee.

To Igierne, Aquae Sulis had always seemed an outpost of civility and culture in the midst of the wild hills. The warm stone of the temple of Sulis and the enclosure surrounding the baths in the center of the city glowed in the afternoon sunshine, and the tiled roofs of the Roman buildings around them had the mellow beauty of an earlier age. Even the Saxon war had not really touched it, though the land to the north had been trampled and torn by the two armies. Igierne had wept, passing the twin mounds where they had burned the bodies of the slain Britons and those of their foes. In life, she reflected, they had been enemies, but in death they all fed the same soil.

The Saxons had kicked down a few doors when they searched Aquae Sulis for foodstuffs, but by Artor's order, the town had been stripped of booty and abandoned before the armies arrived. If the place had not been full of wounded soldiers, she might never have guessed there had been a war.

Those fighters who were still fit to travel were already off to their homes, or harrying the retreating Saxons. Most of the warriors who had been badly wounded were dead. Those who remained in Aquae Sulis had wounds which were not severe enough to kill them outright but required a longer convalescence. The minerals in the water healed torn flesh as its warmth eased aching muscles, and each morning the altar of Sulis bore new offerings.

At dawn, before the day's complement of wounded came to seek the goddess, Igierne and her women visited the baths. Some of the hot and cold pools that had been added to the facilities in the previous century were no longer usable, but the rectangular great bath was still protected by its vaulted ceiling. Seen through the steam that rose from the surface, the marble gods stationed around the pool seemed to nod and sway. Cradled in the warmth of the water, Igierne saluted them: Venus and Mercurius, Jupiter and Juno and Minerva, Ceres and Bacchus, Apollo and his sister Diana with her leaping deer.

Only Mars was missing from this place of healing. But on Mons Badonicus the Britons had made offerings enough to the god of war. Not only Oesc, but Ceretic, the leader of the West Saxons, had fallen there. Aelle, who had led the rebellion, was an old man. It would be a generation or more before the Saxons could hope to field such an army again.

Afterwards, relaxed and glowing, she joined Artor for breakfast in the house of the chief magistrate.

"You look well," he said as they sat down.

"I wish I could say the same for you," she answered. In the pitiless illumination of morning the lines that pain had drawn around his mouth and responsibility had graven on his brow showed even more clearly than they had by torchlight the night before. "You look as if you had lost the war."

"I lost a lot of good men," he said tonelessly. He had filled his bowl with porridge, but he was not eating it. "I lost Oesc."

"He was your enemy!"

Artor shook his head. "Never that. If I had not failed him, there would have been no war. I killed him," he said flatly.

"Not in hatred or anger . . ." she objected softly.

Her son sighed. "I was spared that, at least. It was by his request. His back was broken in the battle, and he wished the mercy stroke to come from my hand."

Igierne considered him, frowning. *You are wounded too, my son, as sorely as any of those men I saw outside the baths.*

"When Uthir died," she said slowly, "I saw no reason to go on. Morgause did not need me, and I did not know where you were. I was no longer a queen. It took time for me to understand that there was still a role for me to play, and things I was needed to do."

"Indeed . . ." Artor breathed, "I felt your presence on the battlefield. And then—" a memory of wonder flared briefly in his eyes "—the goddess came, Sulis Minerva, or Brigantia

Herself, filling our hearts with fire. Britannia owes a great debt to the women of the Holy Isle."

"And now you need me again—" she said, not quite questioning. He did not answer. His face was grim, and she realized that he was not seeing her at all. "Artor," she said sharply, "why did you summon me here?"

"I do need you." His face brightened with a rueful smile. "There remains one task that is too much for my courage. Only a woman—a priestess—can help me now."

Igierne set down her tea and looked at him expectantly.

"I swore to Oesc that I would bury his ashes beside Hengest's mound . . . and I promised to see his wife and infant son back to Cantium."

"Cataur will give her up to you?"

"Has already given—" Artor said grimly, "which is the only reason his head is still connected to his shoulders. Enough Saxon blood has been spilled to satisfy even the Dumnonians. Rigana and her child are safe now at Dun Tagell. I want you to go there and escort her home."

Igierne sat back in her chair, staring, her mind awhirl with memory. "I have not seen Dun Tagell since your father took me away to be married, after Gorlosius died. . . ."

After a moment she realized how much of that ancient grief and anger must have shown in her face by its reflection in Artor's eyes.

"Does it get any easier, Mother? Do the rage and the sorrow fade in time?" he asked then.

"They do . . ." she said slowly, "if you seek healing; if from the destruction you build something new."

He nodded, still holding her gaze. "Healing is what we all need now. After so many years of warfare, Britannia, bruised and battered as she is, knows peace at last. The Sword and the Spear must be put to rest. It is time to bring forth the Cauldron and use its power."

"And for that you need the Lady of the Lake," answered Igierne, "I understand. But you also need a queen."

"Still trying to marry me off, Mother?" The pain lines vanished in a brief grin. "Well, perhaps you are right. I will arrange to visit Leodegranus—after I have confirmed Oesc's son as lord of Cantium."

"So—did Artor send you because he was afraid to face me?" Rigana turned, skirts flaring as the sea breeze caught them, but then there was always wind at Dun Tagell.

"There are a great many demands on the High King's time," Igierne answered neutrally.

"Oh, indeed!" Rigana took a quick step away from the cliff's edge, brown curls blowing across her face and head cocked like an angry bird. "Too many for him to pay attention when that bastard Cataur abducted me, and far too many for him to take the time to rescue me! I would still have a husband, and you would not have had this war, if there had not been so many demands on your son's time!"

Igierne took a firm hold on her own temper. "The women of Demetia whom he saved from slavery in Eriu might not agree with you, but hindsight is a wonderful counselor." She had met Oesc a time or two when he was Artor's hostage, and thought him a pleasant, if rather dour, young man. How had he ended up married to this virago? "He sent me because I know what it is to lose a husband," she continued. "Artor will be waiting for us in Cantium."

"With Oesc's ashes." Rigana's narrow shoulders slumped. "At night I lie awake, remembering all our bitter words. And yet I loved the man, even though he was Saxon and the heir of my family's ancient enemy."

"Artor loved him too," said Igierne quietly.

Together, the two women started along the path that wound about the edge of the rock. The stone wall was low here, a protection for those inside rather than a defense, for no boat could live among the rocks at the base of the sheer cliff that faced the dancing glitter of the sea. They picked their way thorugh the tumbled remains of beehive-shaped huts where monks had lived until Gorlosius turned Dun Tagell into a guardpost, following the curve of the rock back towards the hall.

"Oesc trusted him—" Rigana said bitterly. "He would not

have turned against his own folk for my sake, but I think he might have done so, if Artor had called."

"He went to war with Artor for your sake," Igierne reminded her.

"Do you think I haven't blamed myself for that, too?"

"Blame Cataur—"

"Who goes unpunished!" Rigana exclaimed.

"Not entirely. I am told he will never sit a horse again."

"Artor should have killed him! He taunted me—called me a whore who had sold out to my country's enemy for the sake of a warm bed and a crimson gown!"

They had stopped once more. Below them the sea shone luminous as emerald in the slack water by the shore.

"He wanted to," answered Igierne, "but he needed Cataur's men. The greater good outweighed the desire for revenge—a lesson you will have to learn if you are to hold Cantium until your son is grown."

"Is *that* what Artor intends?" Rigana's eyes widened.

"Cantium is the Eastern Gate of Britannia. Artor trusted Oesc to hold it for him, and promised it to Oesc's son. You are of the old blood of the land. Until Eormenric comes of age, you will be Cantium's queen. You will have to choose a good man to lead the house-guard—" She stopped, for Rigana was not listening.

Overhead gulls darted and soared, squabbling. Rigana had turned towards the hall, and Igierne heard a fainter cry above the mewing of the birds.

"Eormenric—" Rigana crossed her arms above her breasts, where a dark stain was already spreading as her milk let down in response to the baby's cry, and hurried down the path.

Igierne followed more slowly, bracing herself against memories that surged like the waves of the sea. In her mind's eye, the bright afternoon gave way to moonlight, and once more she saw Uthir coming towards her. When a cloaked figure rose up before her, she was not surprised, and reached out eagerly.

"Lady . . . I greet you. . . ."

A woman's voice—Igierne recoiled, blinded by the light of

day. Someone seized her hand and pulled her back to the path, and she stood shaking with reaction.

The woman who was holding her was a little bent, with grey in her hair, wrapped in a grey shawl. It took a moment for Igierne to realize that the glimmer of light around the stranger was no failure of vision, but the aura of power. She took a deep breath, centered herself, and looked again.

"You are Hæthwæge, Oesc's wisewoman," she said then. "Merlin has told me about you."

Hæthwæge smiled, and suddenly she did not seem so old. "And all Britannia knows the Lady of the Lake." Her nod was the salutation of one priestess to another. "I am glad that you have come."

To Igierne's relief, she used the British speech, accented but clear. "Do *you* understand why Artor kept Rigana here?"

The wisewoman's gaze grew bleak. "To keep her safe until Oesc's Wyrd was accomplished. The runes told me what had to be. I loved him dearly, but I knew his life would not be long. Now he goes back to the land."

Igierne looked at her with sudden calculation. That the Saxon woman had power was clear—but what, besides the runes, did she know?

"A time of peace is coming in which our peoples must learn to live together," she said slowly. "And it seems to me that as the years pass, those of us who follow the old ways, both Saxon and Briton, will find we have more in common with each other than we do with the priests of the Christians. You would be welcome at the Lake, to teach our young priestesses, and learn our mysteries."

Hæthwæge stopped short, her gaze gone inward as if she were listening. Then she laughed. "I would like that well, but you must know that where I go, there also goes the god I serve. He has always been very willing to learn from women, and I may teach what I have learned from him. But my duty lies now with Oesc's young son. Until Eormenric is taken from the care of women, I must stay by him. If you are still willing, when that day arrives I will come to you."

"I understand," said Igierne, "and Rigana is fortunate to have you at her side. But we have a journey to make. While we bear each other company, let us share what wisdom we may...."

The harvest was in and the first storm of autumn had swept the west country, cleansing the land and setting the first touch of vivid color in the leaves. But when it was past, the gods seemed to have regretted their threat of winter, for the skies cleared and the air grew warm once more. The Vale of Afallon lay in dreaming peace, and the hills that sheltered it basked beneath the sun.

Even at the villa, where the family of Prince Leodagranus had gone to escape the heat of Lindinis, the air was hot and still. Guendivar, clad in the sheerest linen tunica her mother would permit her, untied the waist cord to let the garment flow freely from the brooches that held it at the shoulders and still felt rivulets of perspiration twining across her skin. Even the wool she was spinning felt slick beneath her fingers. She detached them distastefully and tossed the spindle onto the bench that ran along the covered porch.

Sister Julia started at the clatter, then returned her attention to the even strand that was feeding from the cloud of wool wrapped around her distaff onto her own. She had been Guendivar's constant companion for almost a year, when Petronilla, dazzled by the prospects implied by Queen Igierne's letter, had sent to the Isle of Glass for a nun to guard her daughter's chastity. Mother Maruret had offered them Julia, an orphan of good family who had not yet taken her final vows. She was plain enough to convince Guendivar's mother of her virtue, and at eighteen, young enough so that Guendivar would tolerate her company.

"How can you bear to spin in this weather?" Guendivar exclaimed, resting her hands on the railing and gazing out across the stubble of the hay-meadow. "If they could, I daresay even the sheep would be shedding their fleeces now. But then—" she turned back to Julia "—you always look so cool."

Julia flushed a little, and Guendivar laughed. She had discovered very early that the young woman's fair skin showed every shift in emotion. She was clad, as always, in a gown of heavy undyed linen, and when Guendivar looked more closely, she saw a sheen of perspiration on Julia's brow.

"You *are* hot! Well, that settles it. We are going down to the stream to bathe!"

"But your mother—" Julia stopped her spinning.

"My mother will not be back from Lindinis until tonight, but why should she object? The war is over, and all the lust-crazed soldiers are on their way home!"

It was too bad, really—for all their fears, not one warrior, lusty or not, had come near. It would have brought a little excitement into what had been an anxious but boring summer. Guendivar sighed, knowing her mother would have told her to use the bathhouse attached to the villa, but she saw no reason to make more work for the slaves when what she really wanted was to get out into the woods once more.

Before Julia could protest further, Guendivar had dashed inside for her sandals and some towel cloths and a blanket, and was running down the path. In the next moment, she smiled as she heard the young nun hurrying after her. By now, she had found that within the limitations of her mother's rules, Julia was quite persuadable. Guendivar would even have been glad of her companionship if she could just, once in a while, have spent some time alone.

It had been months since she had had a glimpse of faerie radiance. Did growing up mean that one could no longer see them? But they had *promised* that she would stay the same! Guendivar clung to that knowledge in the lonely nights when she lay awake watching the moon pass her window and listening to Julia's quiet breathing from the other side of the room. Sometimes she thought about simply climbing out the window, but Julia was a light sleeper and would rouse the household to follow her.

But I will do it! she promised herself as she reached the woods and slowed. *No one, not even the High King himself, will keep me locked in for long!*

Julia gave her a reproachful glance as she caught up with her. She was breathing hard and sweating visibly. Guendivar suppressed an impulse of pity. It was Julia's own fault—she knew where Guendivar was going, after all.

But now she could hear the cheerful gurgle of the stream as it purled among the stones of the ford. Below the ford the ground had been cleared so the sheep and the cattle could come down to drink there, but above it, where a screen of alders shaded the water, her father had hollowed out a bathing pool.

Guendivar dropped her towel and stripped off her tunica in a single motion, and made a dash for the pool.

"Oh, it's delicious!" she cried as the coolness closed around her. She ducked beneath the surface and came up laughing, splashed Julia, who had folded her gown and was testing the water with one toe, and laughed again to see it sparkle in the sun. She leaned backward to let the water embrace her and floated, her bright hair raying out around her, her breasts bobbing like pale apples.

Carefully, Julia waded in. Standing, the water lapped her breasts, larger than Guendivar's, though the younger girl was taller, with rosy nipples, erect now in response to the water. Julia's face might be plain, reflected Guendivar, but her body was rounded and beautiful. It was a shame to hide that curving waist beneath a nun's shapeless robe.

She allowed herself to sink beneath the surface once more, turning, opening her legs so the cool water rushed between her thighs. She felt the pressure of the current against her side—or was it the spirit of the pool? Her spirit reached out in wordless longing, and she felt the current curl around her in an insubstantial embrace.

Too soon she had to come up for air, and the moment was gone. She could only be grateful that she was wet already, so Julia could not see her tears. She gathered up her hair and twisted it to wring out the water, then started for the shore.

"Do you want to go back now?" asked Julia. She was washing her hair, black now with moisture, like the delta of shadow between her thighs.

"I will rest awhile and let the air dry me." Guendivar spread out the blanket where the old leaves lay thick beneath the trees and lay down.

Presently Julia joined her, sighing with content as she stretched out at Guendivar's side.

"What is it?" the other girl asked presently. "You look so sad. Is it something I have said or done?"

Damn— thought Guendivar, wiping her eyes. "I used to range the hills like a wild pony! I hate being penned in the house like a mare being kept until the stallion comes. It's not your fault, Julia. You make it almost bearable!"

"Oh, my dear—" Julia reached out to touch her shoulder. "Don't you want to marry the king?"

"He doesn't even know me! Maybe it will come to nothing. Maybe this is all no more than my mother's dream. But if the High King doesn't want me, she will find someone else, and I will be in prison forevermore!"

"Guendivar, it's all right!" murmured Julia, drawing her close as she began to weep once more, holding her pillowed against her soft breast until she had cried herself out and was still.

It had been a long time, thought Guendivar in the peace that followed, since her mother had held her so. Julia's skin was as cool and smooth as her mother's silken gown. Dreamily, as if she were stroking her cat, she slid her fingers down that soft side. Again, and again, she stroked, exploring the contours of muscle and bone beneath the smooth skin, until her hand cupped the curve of the other woman's breast.

Julia gasped, and Guendivar, opening her eyes, saw the betraying flush, rosy as sunrise, beneath the fair skin. "Please—you should not—"

"Touch you? But why not?" asked Guendivar. "Your skin is lovely." She squeezed gently, fingers circling until they found the pink nipple and felt it harden.

"I think . . . it is a sin. . . ." Julia took a quick breath and started to pull away, but Guendivar held her.

"My mother says it is a sin if I let a man touch my body, but you are not a man." Guendivar smiled. "Look, our breasts are nestling together like doves. . . ." She moved closer, feeling a sweet fire begin to burn warm within her own body at the contact of skin on skin. She licked her lips, wondering if that skin would be as sweet to the taste as it was to touch. Julia made a small desperate sound and turned her head away.

"You like me, don't you?" Guendivar asked in sudden doubt. "It's not just because my mother makes you stay—"

"Oh Guendivar, my sweet child, I love you," Julia whispered brokenly, "Didn't you know?" The stiffness went out of her body and she reached up to stroke Guendivar's hair.

"I don't know about love, but I know that you like holding me—" She smiled again and kissed Julia's lips. There was a last moment of resistance, and then the other girl's arms tightened around her.

Together they sank back down on the blanket, and she learned just how much Julia liked her as, clumsy as colts and sensuous as kittens, they discovered the pleasure touch could bring. And presently, lost in sensation, Guendivar forgot the future that prisoned her, and was free.

At Midwinter, the High King came to Lindinis. He was travelling from Londinium to visit Cataur in Isca Dumnoniorum, his message told them, and Lindinis would be a good place to break his journey. He would be there, he said, in time for the festival.

"He has not said he is coming to see *me*," said Guendivar. Scrubbed and scented and swathed in Roman silks, she sat on the chest in her mother's bedchamber, kicking her heels against its carven side.

"He wrote to ask your father if you were spoken for," answered Petronilla, peering into her mirror of polished bronze as she hung discs of gold filigree and garnets in her ears. "God knows how he knew that Leodagranus even *has* a daughter, but if he is coming here, it is you he wants to see. Perhaps he fears that if he marries into Demetia or Dumnonia, the others will be jealous, whereas an alliance with Lindinis will not upset the balance of power. But you come of the blood of the Durotrige princes, and your ancestry is as royal as any in Britannia. So you will be on your best behavior, my girl—" she turned to fix her daughter with a repressive glare "—and show yourself worthy to be Artor's bride."

And why should I want to be a queen? Guendivar wondered mutinously. *From all I have heard, they have even less freedom than other wives*—but she did not say so aloud. Her mother had explained quite clearly the advantages to her family, and threatened to send her back to the Isle of Glass with Julia if she refused.

"At least," Petronilla continued as she settled the veil over her hair, "you are in blooming looks."

Guendivar felt a betraying flush heat her cheeks and hoped her mother would put it down to maidenly modesty. It was Julia's care for her and the joy they had together that had made these past months bearable.

Sounds from the street below brought both of them to their feet, listening. Petronilla moved swiftly to the porch that overlooked the atrium and glanced down.

"They've come—quickly now, we must be ready to greet them—" She reached for her daughter's hand and towed her out of the room.

Guendivar's first thought was that Artor was old. After a second glance, she decided that perhaps he was merely very tired. He was tall and well-muscled, though rather thin, and his brown hair showed only a few threads of grey. He might even be rather good looking, if he ever relaxed. She wondered if she were judging him so harshly because he had hardly looked at her? Once they were all seated in the triclinium and the slaves began to bring in the food, the king had directed all his remarks to her father and brother.

Artor's nephew Gualchmai, an enormous young man who reminded her of a mastiff puppy her brother had once brought home, was doing his best to compensate.

"Those two louts who are swilling at the end of yon table are my brothers Gwyhir and Aggarban—" he said, gesturing broadly, the goblet of pale green glass seeming impossibly fragile in his big hand. "And there's two more at Dun Eidyn still to come."

Guendivar lifted one eyebrow. Gwyhir, sitting beneath the garland of winter greenery that had been draped across the frescoed wall, was almost as tall as his brother, Aggarban shorter and more solid, but still a big man.

"And you go everywhere with the king?" she asked.

"We do, along with Betiver, that narrow dark lad yonder

who is nephew to Riothamus in Gallia, and Cai, who was Artor's foster-brother."

"He has formidable protectors." She saw him blink as she smiled.

"Aye, well—we lost some good men at Mons Badonicus, but seemingly we'll have less need of them from now on." Gualchmai looked as if he were trying to convince himself this was a good thing.

The slaves came in to clear the platters of venison and roast pork away and replace them with honeycakes and pies made from the apples of the vale. Soon the feast would be over. Would the men sit down to their drinking and send the women away? Guendivar no longer wished to avoid Artor; indeed, she had begun to think that if she did not arrange an encounter, she would have no chance to speak with him at all.

"I think my father is about to end the feasting—" she told Gualchmai. "You might tell your lord that even at midwinter I often walk in the atrium at night to breathe the fresh air. . . ."

"A good commander is always glad of information—" He grinned at her approvingly. "I will make certain that he knows."

Well, at least *he* seemed to like her, she thought as she followed her mother out of the room. If Artor did not want her, perhaps she could marry Gualchmai.

It was late, and even the hooded cloak was no longer quite sufficient to keep off the chill, when Guendivar heard a man's step upon the stones. Shivering, she stood up, and saw him stop short, then move slowly forward until he stood before her. She thought for a moment that it might be Gualchmai, come to tell her that Artor would not be there. But those senses with which she had learned to see the folk of faerie identified not the king's appearance but his unique aura of power.

"I am sorry—" he said finally. "I have kept you waiting, and you are cold." He shrugged off his crimson mantle and draped it around her shoulders. It still held the heat of his body and warmed her like a fire.

"But you will be cold—" she protested.

"I've campaigned in worse weather than this, in armor. *That* is cold!"

"I have never been cold without a way to get warm, never marched without food or panted from thirst, never done labor that I could not stop when I willed. Except for spinning, of course—" she added ruefully. He was surprisingly easy to talk to—perhaps it was because she could not see him. They were two spirits, speaking together in the dark.

"What *has* Gualchmai been telling you?" Artor said, on a breath of laughter. "I do not expect my queen to march with the army. I hope that in the next few years even *I* won't have to march with the army, at least not all the time."

"Would you then keep your wife like a jewel in a golden setting?" Guendivar's voice was very soft.

There was another charged silence, then Artor sighed. "Your brother tells me that you are a great rider, and can stay out all day, ranging the hills. I would not cage you, Guendivar, even in gold. If you wish it, I would be glad to have you riding at my side."

She straightened, trying to see his face. She was a tall girl, but still she had to look up at him. "From what Gualchmai says, you are never more than a moon in the same place. I think I will have to—"

"It is a bargain, then?" Relief made his voice unsteady as he set his hands on her shoulders.

"It is—" She had feared this marriage as a prison, but now she was beginning to think it might be an adventure. The pressure of his hands felt warm and secure.

"In the spring, then—" He stopped suddenly. "How old are you?"

"At the beginning of April I will be fifteen." She strove for dignity.

His hands dropped suddenly and he shook his head. "Sweet Goddess! And yet, if I was old enough to be king at that age, I suppose that you can be a queen."

Her assurance left her suddenly. "I will try—"

Artor eased back her hood. He took her face between his hands, gentle as if he were touching a butterfly, and kissed her on the brow.

THE FLOWER BRIDE

A·D· 496

THAT YEAR SPRING CAME EARLY TO BRITANNIA, AS IF THE LAND were adorning itself to celebrate the wedding of the High King. Every dell was scattered with creamy primroses; the woodland rides were flooded with bluebells, and in the hedges the starry white of hawthorn veiled each bough.

As the bridal procession left the Summer Country and made its slow way towards Londinium, folk thronged from tiled villas and thatched Celtic roundhouses, from shepherds' lonely huts and half-ruined towns to hail the bride whose marriage would set a seal of peace upon the land. Surely, they sang, the wars were truly ended, if the High King was at last giving them a queen. Where Guendivar passed, the road was strewn with flowers.

To Merlin, making his way southward from the Caledonian forest, the rumor of her progress was like a warm breath of wind from some fruitful southern land. He found himself hastening, moved by a hope he had not dared to feel for far too long. He had been born to serve the Defender of Britannia and set him on his throne, and he had succeeded in that task. None of them had dared to think about what might come afterward.

But now the land itself was providing the answer. After winter came the spring, after sorrow, this joy, after the death of the Britannia that had been ruled by Rome, a new nation in which all the gathered greatness of the peoples who had settled here could flower.

Igierne, riding south with Ceincair and Morut, could not help but contrast this wedding with her marriage to Uthir, that hurried, makeshift ceremony held in the dead of winter and the aftermath of a civil war to legitimize the child she was already carrying. Guendivar would come to her marriage a virgin, with neither memories of the past nor fears for the future to shadow the day. If the queen mother had not been so profoundly relieved at the prospect of passing on a part of the burden she had carried for so long, she would have envied her son's bride.

For Artor's sister, riding swiftly southward with her escort of Votadini tribesmen, each milestone on the old Roman road was a reminder of her own dilemma. For so long she had told herself that the freedom of a queen in Alba suited her far better than any title dying Britannia had to offer. Now she was about to find out if she really believed it. If Artor had never been born, her own descent from the House of Maximus might have given her husband a claim to torque and diadem. Yet the closer she got to Londinium, the more clearly Morgause understood that it was not Guendivar whom she envied, but Artor himself. She did not desire to be a consort, but the ruling queen.

Even in decline, the Romanized Britons for whom Boudicca was still a name with which to frighten children would never have accepted her. Artor's son would inherit his imperium. The only question was whether that son would be the child of her womb, or Guendivar's.

Artor himself, struggling with questions of personality and precedence, remembered the bright face of the girl he had met at midwinter and wondered if he had the right to plunge any woman into the political morass this wedding had become. Even the choice of a place to hold the ceremony had provoked a battle. Bishop Dubricius had offered his own church in Isca, but to marry there would have insulted the Dumnonians, already on the defensive because they were blamed for provoking the last Saxon war.

Artor could have been married in the bride's home, but Lindinis was only a secondary tribal civitas, and had no edifice large enough to hold all those who would want to come. Calleva or Sorviodunum were central, but too closely associated with the wars. At least Londinium had once been the country's undisputed capital, and in the basilica and the Palace of the Governors there would be room for all.

But as the first of May drew closer Artor would have been glad of an excuse to send some of them home again. Planning battles was much easier. He was beginning to think that the ancient custom of marriage by capture had a lot to recommend it. Guendivar had said she liked to ride—perhaps she would prefer being carried off. But when the king tried this theory out on his companions, they only laughed. Gualchmai, who had more experience with women than any three of the rest of them, assured him that women *liked* ceremonies with flowers and candles and uncomfortable new clothes.

As for Guendivar herself, she rode through the blossoming landscape in a haze of delight, accepting the gifts men brought her and the homage they paid her beauty; exulting in the movement of the horse beneath her, the brightness of the sunlight and the sweetness of the flowers. Focused on the excitement of each moment, she scarcely thought about the wedding towards which this journey was leading her.

"Old Oesc used to say these walls were like the work of etins—titans . . ." said Betiver, gesturing at the ruins of the gatehouse that had once guarded the Calleva Road. The rubble had been cleared away, but the gate had never been repaired.

Guendivar gazed around her with interest as they passed. "It looks old, and sad. Will Artor rebuild it?"

"Why should he trouble himself," asked Gualchmai, laughing, "when the walls are as full of holes as a cloak when the moths have been making free? Walls!" He made a rude gesture. "No good are they without brave men and sharp spears behind them!"

"Oh, indeed," said his brother Gwyhir, who rode just behind him, "and you yourself are as good as an army!"

Guendivar laughed. After three weeks on the road, she had
taken their measure. Artor had sent the youngest and liveliest
of his Companions to be her escort, and they had preened
and pranced for her from Lindinis to Londinium. They reminded her of puppies showing off, even Betiver, who was
said to have a permanent mistress in the town and a nine-
year-old son.

"The high roof you see belongs to the basilica," he told her.
"That is where the wedding feast will be—I think it is the
only building in Britannia large enough to hold all the people
Cai has invited. The church is nearer the river."

"And the palace?"

"Beyond the basilica, on the other side of the square. Of
course only the main wing is still usable, but with luck, we'll
be able to find enough sound roofs in Londinium to keep
everyone dry!" He sent a suspicious glance skyward, but the
overcast did not look as if it were going to deepen into rain.

Guendivar sighed. She had looked forward to staying in a
palace, but this vast city, its old buildings leprous with decay,
held little of the splendour of her dreams. Ghosts might dwell
here, but not the folk of faerie. She thought wistfully of the
fields through which they had passed to come here, adorned
more richly than any work of the Romans with spring flowers.

But she must not let her escort sense her unease. "Is Artor
here already?" she asked brightly. "Will he come to greet
me?"

The Votadini brothers turned to Betiver, who replied with
a wry smile, "I am sure that so soon as he knows you have
arrived he will come to you—but as for where he is now—
well, you will learn soon enough that Artor is not one for
sitting still."

But the High King was not working. Igierne had arrived
the previous day and, finding her son in the old office of the
procurator, surrounded by scraps of paper, had carried him
off to the river. As a boy he had learned the difficult art of

paddling a coracle; she pressed him into service now as her boatman and ordered him to take her upstream.

High clouds had spread a silver veil partway across the heavens. Each stroke of the paddle set reflections rippling like pearl. From time to time some other craft, coming downstream, would pass them. Igierne lifted a hand to answer their hails, but Artor had not the breath to reply.

She watched him with a critical eye, noting the flex and stretch of muscle in his arms and back as he drove the round skin-covered craft against the current. Sometimes an eddy would spin them, and Artor needed all of his strength as well as skill to get them back on course. He was sweating freely by the time she told him to stop.

The coracle spun round once more, then began to drift gently back towards the city whose smoke hazed the river below them like a shadow of the clouds. Artor rested the paddle on his knees, still breathing hard.

"Do you feel better?" she asked.

For a moment he stared; then his exasperation gave way to wonder.

"In fact, I do . . ."

"There is nothing like vigorous action to relieve strain, and you have been under a great deal, my child." He spent much time outdoors and his color was good, but she noticed more than one thread of silver in the brown hair, and there were new shadows around his eyes.

"I have never been required to plan a campaign of peace before," he said apologetically. "In war it is easy. If a man has a sword at your throat, he is an enemy. Here, I have only allies, who think they know what is needed better than I. I might believe them—if they could only all agree!"

Igierne laughed. "It is not so different among my priestesses on the Isle of Maidens." For a few moments they were silent, watching the ducks dive into the reedbeds as they passed. Then she spoke once more. "Tell me, is it easier to move the boat upstream or down?"

"Down, of course," he answered, one brow lifting in enquiry.

"Just so. Think—is not everything easier when you move with the current instead of fighting it?"

He nodded. "Like charging downhill."

"Like this wedding—" she said then. "Guendivar is the woman whom the fates have ordained for you. To make her your wife you don't have to fight the world. Let it be. Relax and allow her to come to you." She stopped suddenly. "Or are you afraid?"

He knew how to govern his face, but she saw his knuckles whiten as he gripped the oar.

"She is so young, Mother. She has never heard the ravens singing on a battlefield, or seen the life ebb from the face of a man you love. She has never known how fury can seize you and make you do terrible things, conscious of nothing until you come to yourself and see the blood on your hands. What can I say to her? What kind of a life can we have?"

"A life of peace," answered his mother, "though you will not have done with battles entirely while the Picts still ride southward and Eriu sends warriors across the sea. It is because she is innocent that you need this girl. You need say nothing—let her talk to you. . . . She will be Tigernissa, High Queen. Men fight for land, but the life of the land is in the waters that flow through it. The power of the waters belongs to the queen. It is for her to initiate you into its mysteries."

A gull swooped low, yammering, and when it saw they had no food, soared away. They could smell woodsmoke now, and on the shore the wharves of Londinium were beginning to come into view.

"The river has great power. See how swiftly we have returned? Beneath all the eddies, all the flotsam that rides its surface and the ruffling of the wind, the deep current of the river rolls. It is the same with the squabbles of humankind. Worship as you must for Britannia's peace, but never forget how strong these waters are as they move so steadily toward the sea. . . ."

The night before the wedding it rained. At dawn, clouds still covered the sky, but as they thinned, they admitted a little watery sunshine. When Guendivar came out of the palace, the wet stones of the pavement were shining. She gazed around her, blinking at the brightness. At that moment, even this place of wood and stone was beautiful. Her escort was already formed up and waiting. When they saw her, they began to cheer, drowning out the clamor that marked the progress of the groom's procession, already two streets away.

Her mother twitched at the hawthorn wreath that held the bridal veil. Its fiery silk had been embroidered with golden flowers. More flowers were woven into the crimson damask of her dalmatic and worked into its golden borders in pearls. Jewels weighted the wide neckband and the strip of gold that ran from throat to hem. It was a magnificent garment, fit for an empress of the eastern lands from which it had come— everyone said so. But it was so heavy Guendivar could hardly move.

Her mother gripped her elbow, pulling her forward. For a moment Guendivar resisted, filled with a wild desire to strip down to her linen undergown and make a dash for the open fields. How could they praise her beauty when her body was encased in jewels like a relic and her face curtained by this veil? It was an image they shouted for, like the icon of the Virgin that was carried in procession at festivals.

But she had given her word to Artor.

"She comes! She comes—" cried the crowd "—the Flower Bride!"

Stiff as a jointed puppet, Guendivar mounted the cart, its railings wound with primroses and violets and its sides garlanded with eglantine. As it passed through the streets, people strewed the road with all the blooms of May. They brightened the way, but could not soften the rough stones. Guendivar gripped the rail, swaying as the cart jolted forward.

They turned a corner and came into the square before the church, a modest whitewashed structure dwarfed by what remained of the imperial buildings that still surrounded it. The hills of the Summer Country seemed very far away.

The groom's escort was already drawn up beside it, and the bishop waited before the church door, his white vestments as heavily ornamented as her gown. Even Artor was cased in cloth of gold that glittered in the pale sunlight. *We are all images*, she told herself, *existing only to play our roles in this ceremony*. But what force could manipulate kings for its pleasure? The people, perhaps? Or their gods?

The cart halted. Guendivar allowed them to help her descend, and her father, grinning as if she were his sole invention, led her to the church door. Marriages were blessed by the Church, but they were not part of its liturgy. Still, the porch of the church seemed a strange place for a ceremony. Through the haze of silk she could see Artor, looking as stiff and uncomfortable as she. Bishop Dubricius cleared his throat, gathering the attention of the crowd.

"In nomine Patris, et Filii, et Espiritu Sancti—"

Guendivar felt her heart beat like that of a trapped hare as the sonorous Latin rolled on, a river of words that was sweeping her and Artor both away.

Only when the sound ceased did she rouse. Everyone was looking at her, waiting for her answer. Could she, even now, refuse? But as she gazed frantically around her the sun broke through the clouds, and suddenly all the world was a glitter of light. She shut her eyes against that brilliance, but behind her eyelids it still blazed.

"Volo—" she heard her own voice say.

There were more words, and then the deep murmur of Artor's reply. The priest bound their hands, turned them to show themselves to the people, whose joyous response smote the sky.

Then Artor led her into the darkness of the church for the nuptial mass.

The scent of flowers hung heavy in the hall, mingling unpleasantly with the odors of human sweat and spilled wine. From the high table on the dais at the end of the basilica, tables had been set end to end in front of the walls. Upon the benches of the king's side, all the princelings of Britannia, and on the queen's side, their wives and daughters, sat packed like pickles in a crock.

Morgause took another drink from her own cup, breathing deep to let the sharp fumes drive the other scents away. When the last of the Roman governors abandoned his post, the items he had left behind included some amphoras of good wine. It was a little past its prime—Artor had been right to use it now. She sighed, aware that the wine was making her melancholy. When she was a girl they had drunk wine like this in her father's hall, but in times to come they would have to swill like barbarians on mead and heather beer.

A clatter of steel on shield leather brought everyone upright as the sword dancers marched in. Some of the male guests leaped from their benches, reaching as if they expected to find their own weapons hanging behind them on the wall. Morgause grinned sourly. These were the champion dancers among her husband's tribesmen; it pleased her to see these fat southern lords, if only for a moment, feel afraid.

The dancers' tunics, though clean, were of rough wool, and the earthy hues woven into their mantles dull against the bright colors of the princes, but their swords flashed in the torchlight. Singing, they formed two squares. Shields lifted into position, and they began their deadly play.

The singers who had been performing earlier had almost been drowned out by the hum of conversation, but the sword dancers riveted everyone's attention. Even the little bride, who had been picking at the slice of roast boar with which Artor had served her, put down her knife to stare.

"They are Votadini?" asked the woman beside Morgause. She was called Flavia, invited because she had been foster-mother to Artor.

She nodded. "They come from a clan on our border with Alta Cluta."

"They are most . . . energetic . . ." Flavia replied. "Your husband must be proud. But I do not see him. Is he well?"

"Well enough," answered Morgause tightly, "but his joints pain him too much to make such a journey."

"Ah, I understand—" Flavia grimaced in sympathy. "I came in a horselitter, and still it was two days before I could walk without wincing! It is the price of growing old. Of course *you* are still young—" she said after an uncomfortable moment had passed.

Morgause thought of her own aches and kept silence. On

her other side the mothers of the bride and groom were deep in conversation. Morgause had stopped resenting having to sit below Guendivar's mother, when she realized that Petronilla, puffed with pride though she might be, would save her from having to talk to Igierne.

"And what do you think of our new queen?" asked Flavia.

Morgause bared her teeth in a smile. "She is pretty enough, but very young—"

Young enough to be Artor's daughter, if he had been married off at the age I was. Young enough to be a sister to Artor's son. . . . Medraut had begged to come with her to the wedding. He was quite self-possessed for a nine-year-old—she had trained him well, but instinct counselled her to wait. Medraut's time was yet to come.

"But you yourself were married at much the same age, were you not, and to a much older man?" Flavia commented, far too acutely.

And now I am tied to an ancient who is good for nothing but to sit by the fire, while I am still in my prime! Morgause thought then. It would serve Guendivar right if she found herself in the same situation with Artor. It could happen—Leudonus was proof that some warriors lived to be old.

"It is not her age but her intelligence that will make the difference," Morgause answered tartly. "A pretty face alone will not hold a man's interest for long."

"Then we must hope that she can do so, for my Arktos was always a conscientious lad, and I suspect he will remain faithful, whether she loves him or no."

Morgause regarded her thoughtfully. Igierne, for all her lofty sentiments, knew less of her son than this woman who had raised him. She leaned forward until she could see the middle of the table. The bride had given up all pretense of eating and was looking distinctly uncomfortable. Her face was flushed as if she had drunk more than she was used to. Morgause suppressed a smile.

Carefully she swung her legs over the bench and stood. "It is time I visited the privies," she said loudly. "Would anyone like to keep me company?"

Guendivar's eyes focused suddenly. "I would! If I drink any more I will burst!"

Petronilla looked pained, but she assisted the bride to disentangle her robes and rise. There was anxiety in Igierne's eyes as as well, but what could be more natural than for a sister-in-law to escort the new queen?

Artor looked up, smiling with friendly concern. His companions had been seated at a lower table, but Gualchmai had left his place and was leaning with his arm draped across the top of the king's chair. He nodded politely to his mother, but his eyes were watchful. Morgause smiled blandly and took Guendivar's arm.

The old Roman lavatory facilities were still in use. Beyond them, a corridor opened out onto the colonnade. When they had finished and washed, Morgause paused.

"The air in the hall was so hot and warm; I still feel a little faint. Will you bear me company for a few moments in the fresh air?"

"Gladly—" answered Guendivar. "I had been hoping for a chance to speak with you," she added shyly. "You are still a reigning queen. I suspect there are things you can tell me that I will need to know."

Morgause peered at her through the darkness Shouts of laughter echoed faint from the hall. Could the child possibly be as ingenuous as she sounded?

"Do you love Artor?" she asked suddenly.

There was a constricted silence. "I agreed to marry him. I will do my best to make him happy."

Morgause considered. In these garments the girl looked like an overdressed doll, but she had good bones, and her hair, a reddish gold that curled to her waist, was beautiful. Did Artor want an ally or an adorer? If he had chosen Guendivar for her pretty face, she would not hold his interest for long.

Duty was an unexciting bedfellow, but a good companion. What would this girl find it hardest to give? It occurred to her that it would serve Medraut better if Artor did not find too much comfort in his queen.

"My brother is not a bad man," she said thoughtfully, "but he has been a king as long as you have been alive. He is accustomed to obedience. And he has been at war for many years. He will want diversion. Amuse him—be playful—feign passion, even if you do not feel it. And if he seems cold, well, you will be surrounded by virile young men. If you are discreet, you can use them for your pleasure. It has worked well for me."

And that was true enough. But Artor was not Leudonus, who had known very well that his marriage was a political alliance, and never expected more. In Alba, the lustiness of the queen was as important as that of the king. And Alba was not a Christian land.

"You are young," said Morgause, "and know little of the body's demands. But as you mature you will find that a woman has needs too, and kings are very busy men. . . ."

A door opened and light and shadow barred the colonnade.

"They have missed us," Guendivar said quickly. "We had better go in—"

"But of course," answered Morgause. "You are the queen, and you command." But as she followed Guendivar back into the hall, she was smiling.

A murmur of appreciation greeted Guendivar's entrance. Morgause hung back a little, noting the gleam in men's eyes as they watched her come. This one would not have to entice men to her bed if she decided she wanted them—they would be lining up at her door. The remains of the feast lay about them like a looted battlefield. Men had drunk enough now to want something else, and tonight, all their lust was projected upon the king.

"Don't you think it time the little bride was bedded?" she said to Gualchmai as she passed. "She is ready, and he should not make her wait too long."

Some of the other men heard and began to bang their mugs against the planks of the table. "To bed, to bed—let Artor prove that he is king!"

Guendivar's face was nearly as scarlet as her gown, but even the women were laughing.

"Very well," said Petronilla with what dignity she could muster. "Come, ladies, let us escort the queen to the bridal chamber and make her ready for her husband."

Shouting and singing, the women crowded around the new queen and bore her away. But Morgause remained, waiting in the shadow of a pillar as the masculine banter became ever more explicit, until the king was blushing almost as hotly as his bride.

Presently she saw the little nun who had been Guendivar's chaperone returning to tell them she was ready.

The men, for a moment abashed by her grave gaze, grew quieter. Morgause stepped forward.

"And will you also, sister, wish me joy?" Artor asked. "I thought you would be with the women who are helping Guendivar—"

"Oh, I have given her my advice already—" answered Morgause.

"And have you any counsel for me? Your sons have been as frank as farmers with suggestions on how I should practice a husband's craft."

If he had not mentioned her sons, perhaps, even then, Morgause would have kept silent. But she smiled and slid her hand gently along his upper arm.

"But you already know how to deal with a woman, dear brother, *don't you remember?*" she said very softly. "And you have a son to prove it, begotten ten years since at the feast of Lugus. His name is Medraut." Still smiling, she took his face between her hands and kissed him.

His lips were cold, and as she released him, she saw, bleak as the morning after battle, the dawn of desolation in his eyes.

The bed linen smelled of lavender. Guendivar ran her hands across the cloth, smooth with many launderings, and sighed. The linen was old, like this chamber, whose stones seemed to whisper tales of those who had lain here in the years since the mud huts of the Trinovantes were replaced by the stone and plaster of Rome.

She sat up, wrapping her arms around her knees. *What am I doing here?* She belonged in the open land of wood and field, not in this box of stone. Even the silk nightrobe in which they had wrapped her seemed alien. Weather permitting, she preferred to sleep bare. She considered pulling the garment off, but her mother had impressed upon her the need to behave modestly—it would never do to shock her new husband, after all.

Guendivar found it hard to believe that a man who had been living in military camps for half his life would be disturbed by bare skin. Did Artor really believe that she was the simpering maiden her mother had counselled her to be? She tried to remember their single conversation—it had seemed to her then that it was because she had red blood in her veins that he had liked her.

As she started to untie the neckstrings she heard shouting from the corridor and her fingers stilled. They were coming. Suddenly the garment seemed not a constriction, but protection. She pulled up the bedclothes and sat staring as the door swung open and torchlight, dimming the flicker of the lamps, streamed into the room.

The doorway filled with faces, their laughter faltering as they saw her sitting there. For a moment she saw herself with their vision: eyes huge in her white face, mantled in shining hair.

The crowd heaved as the men who were behind pushed forward, then moved aside to admit a figure that moved in a haze of gold, from the band around his brows to the embroidery on his mantle. But his face was in shadow, and though he was surrounded by a leaping, laughing crowd, his stillness matched her own.

"The way is clear!" came Gualchmai's shout. "Get in with you, man—I'll cover you!"

"Nay, it is Artor who will be covering his bride!" someone replied, and the hall rang with masculine laughter. They sounded like her brother and his friends when they had been drinking.

"For shame, lads—give the man some privacy!" That came from Betiver.

Morgause would have known how to command those boors to leave them. Guendivar recalled the Votadini queen's words to her and felt her skin grow hot with remembered embarrassment—perhaps Artor's sister would not have cared.

Then Artor turned to face his tormentors. Their laughter

faded, and she wondered what they were seeing in his eyes. He swung round, and a long stride carried him over the threshold. His arm swept out and the heavy door slammed behind him.

The noise outside fell suddenly to a murmur; she thought they were singing and was glad she could not distinguish the words. Inside, the dark shape by the door seemed to gather silence around him until it was a palpable weight in the air. Guendivar drew the bedclothes closer, shivering. She had not expected her new husband to leap upon her, but why was he still standing there? Could he possibly be afraid?

When the silence had become more disturbing than anything she could imagine him doing, she cleared her throat.

"I do not know the etiquette of these things, but the priests assure me that you have a right to be here. Are you waiting for an invitation to lie down with me?"

Some of the tension went out of him and he laughed. "Perhaps I am. I will confess to you, Guendivar, that I have more experience in 'these things' than you do, but not . . . much—" His voice cracked. "I have a son."

She lifted an eyebrow. "Before he was married my father got three, and for all I know, more afterward. Did you think I would be scandalized?"

And yet it was strange that the High King could have a child that no one had heard of. Bastards begotten before marriage were not unusual, and for a man, no shame. If Morgause was to be believed, in Alba they were not shameful for a woman either, but this was hardly the moment to say so. For a moment she longed for the comfort of Julia's warm arms, even though she knew that for every hour they had lain together the other girl had spent three on her knees. It had always seemed strange to Guendivar to do penance for something that gave the same simple pleasure as a cat arching to the stroke of a caress, but at least she understood what Julia wanted when she was in her arms.

This male creature that radiated tension from the doorway was totally strange, but clearly, if she did not do something, he might well stand there until dawn.

"I am told that you begin by taking off your clothes," she

said wryly. "Do you need help? It took three women to get me out of mine."

Artor laughed again, as if she had surprised him, and shook his head. But he did unbuckle his belt and then the brooch that held his mantle at the shoulder. The rustle of heavy silk seemed loud in the quiet of the room.

"And what do you suggest I do next?" he asked when he was down to the twist of linen about his loins.

Surely, she thought with an unexpected lift of the heart, that had been amusement she heard in his tone. But why should he need to ask? Did he really believe that one bastard had made him unfit to approach her?

"Next, you get into the bed . . ."

He drew a quick breath, and she had a sudden insight into how he must look before battle. She hoped he did not see her as an enemy. She twitched the covers aside and the leather straps of the bedstead creaked as he lay down. In the flicker of lamplight she could see the curves and planes of his body quite clearly. Except for his face and forearms, his skin was almost as fair as her own, scrolled here and there by the subtle pink or silvery tracery of old battle scars. She stared curiously. She had seen men's bodies before, stripped for labor in the fields or exposed to piss against a tree, but never at such close quarters.

After a moment she realized that Artor's breathing was too controlled. What was wrong? He hadn't been so tense when they talked at midwinter. Even this morning there had been open friendliness in his smile. This was not how she had imagined her wedding night would be.

"You did not marry me for love but because you needed an heir," Guendivar said finally. "So far as I know, there is only one way to get one. You may have a son, but he cannot inherit from you, so let us be about it. It would be a pity to disappoint all those people I hear making noise to encourage us out there!"

Artor turned, raising himself on one elbow to look at her. "I have been misled—men always speak of women as if they were creatures of flight and fancy, but I see it is not so—" He took her hand, callused fingers tracing spirals across her palm.

Guendivar drew a quick breath, all her senses focusing on his touch, from which warmth had begun to radiate in little bursts of sparks across her skin. *The female animal desires the male . . .* she told herself, *so why should I be surprised?* If they did not have love, lust was no bad foundation for a marriage, so long as it came linked with laughter. For surely there was nothing here to match the ecstasy she had found in the company of the faerie-folk, but she had not expected it.

"If it were, how could you trust us to manage your homes and raise your children?" she asked tartly, and then, while she still had the courage, lifted his hand and pressed it to her breast.

As his fingers tightened, the sparks became a flame that leaped from nipple to nipple and focused in a throbbing ache between her thighs. Her play with Julia had awakened her body, and since they began this wedding journey there had been no way for them to be alone. If Artor was surprised, his changed breathing told her that the fire had kindled him as well.

She slid her hands from his shoulders down the hard muscle of his sides. Were men's and women's bodies so different? Heart pounding, she brushed upward across his nipples and heard him gasp. Guendivar smiled then, and reached down to tug at his clout. Artor tensed, but at least he did not pull away, and when she eased back down on the bed he came with her, his movement pushing her gown above her thighs.

She could feel his male member hard against her and wished she could see it, but at last he was kissing her. Guendivar held him tightly, a part of her mind cataloguing the differences between his hard strength and Julia's yielding softness, while the remainder was being consumed by an expanding flame.

Artor pushed against her and she opened her thighs, trembling with mingled excitement and fear. This, certainly, was something she had not experienced with Julia! His hands tightened painfully on her shoulders and he thrust again. She felt a tearing pain, them the pressure abruptly eased. He continued to batter against her for a few moments longer, but it was with his body only—the part that had taken her maidenhead slid free, and she had not the art to arouse it again.

Presently he stilled and collapsed onto the bed beside her, breathing hard.

"Was it like this," she said softly when he was still, "when you begot your son?"

"I do not know ... I do not remember..." he groaned, "but it cannot have been," he added bitterly, "or there would have been no child ..."

Only then did she understand that the act had been incomplete for him as well.

"Dear God!" He turned onto his back and she saw that he was weeping. "What have I done? What did she do to me?"

Guendivar let out her breath in a long sigh. She would not, she gathered, come from this night with child. She sensed the pain in the man beside her without understanding it.

"It will be all right," she said presently, "we have time."

Gradually the rasp of his breathing slowed. "Time ..." he groaned. "Ten years ..."

Guendivar touched his shoulder, but he did not respond. After that, they were silent. Even the noise outside their door had ceased. The place between her thighs throbbed with a mingling of pleasure and pain. Presently she pulled the covers over her, and used her hand to release the tension Artor's touch had aroused.

Her husband lay very still beside her, and if he realized what she was doing, he made no sign.

That night, while Artor's Companions were finishing off the last of the Procurator's wine, the mother of his son lay in the arms of a lusty guardsman in a union which, however unblessed, was considerably more rewarding. Igierne slept alone in the room she had once shared with Uthir, plagued by troubled dreams. But Merlin watched out the night at the top of the ancient guard tower, striving to understand the portents he glimpsed in the stars, and in the church where Guendivar had been married, Julia lay stretched upon the cold stones, wrestling with her soul in prayer.

THE SACRED ROUND

A·D· 497

Camalot SMELLED OF RAW WOOD AND RANG WITH THE sound of hammers. It seemed to have grown every time the king's household returned to it, the timber and stone ramparts raised higher, the framing of the great henge hall and the other buildings more solid against the spring sky. The hill had been part of Guendivar's dowry, and if the past year had seen little progress in the intimate side of their marriage, externally, Artor had accomplished a great deal.

From the timber guard tower above the southwest gate the queen saw small figures of men and horses climbing the road. That would be Matauc of Durnovaria—she recognized the standard. He was an old man now, and Artor had not been sure he would come. No doubt curiosity had brought him, as it had so many others—Britannia was full of tales about the new stronghold Artor was building in Leodagranus' land.

Most of the other princes were here already—the place was full of men and horses, and the clusters of hide tents and brushwood bothies that sheltered their escorts nestled close to the wall. According to Leodagranus, it had been a Durotrige fortress when the Romans came, destroyed in the years after Boudicca's war, and then it had been the site of a pagan shrine. But Merlin said the Durotriges were only the latest of the peoples who had sheltered on the hill, tribes now so long gone that no one even remembered their names.

Cai had laughed at him, for on first sight its tree-choked slopes seemed no different from any of the surrounding hills. But when they reached the summit, they found a roughly flattened oblong with a swell of earth around it, and three additional ramparts carved into the side of the hill. The trees they cut to clear the site had provided timber to brace the rubble wall and planks for the breastwork that topped it.

Guendivar climbed the ladder from the sentry walk to the gatehouse often. Here, she could lean on the wickerwork railing and watch the bustle without being overwhelmed by it, and there was usually a breeze. Gazing out across the tree-clad hills she could almost imagine herself free.

Below her, men were setting more stones into the rough facing of the rampart. Just because Artor had called a consilium did not mean work could cease. From here Camalot was a place of circles within circles: the ramparts that ringed the hill, and the huts within the wall, and in the space to the east of the more conventional rectangular building where Artor had his quarters, the great henge hall.

In truth, it was not so much a hall as a shelter, for sections of its wickerwork walling could be removed to let in light and air. Its design had also been one of Merlin's suggestion, neither a Roman basilica nor even a Celtic roundhouse, although it most resembled the latter. Merlin said it was another inspiration from ancient days. The thatched roof was supported on a triple henge of stout wooden pillars, its diameter so great that a hundred and fifty warriors could sit in a circle around the central fire. The old sorcerer still made Guendivar uneasy, but there was no denying his ideas were sometimes useful.

She turned and saw the gate guard lifting an earthenware jug to his lips.

"Is that wine?" she asked, feeling suddenly dry.

The man blushed—surely he should have been accustomed to her by now. "Oh no, lady—'tis water only. My lord king would have my ears did I drink while on guard. But you're welcome to share it—" he added, flushing again. He wiped the rim of the jug with the hem of his tunic and offered it to her.

She eyed it a little dubiously, for his tunic was not over-clean, but she could not insult him by refusing it now. And the water was good, kept cold by the clay. She savored it, rolling it on her tongue, before swallowing. When she had drunk, she handed back the jug and smiled, a thirst that no water could ease fed by the admiration with which he gazed back at her. Tomorrow at the council she would see her beauty reflected in the gleam of other men's eyes.

A hail from below brought her around. She leaned over the railing and waved at Betiver, who had been sent to escort Matauc to the hill. The first gate had opened, and Betiver, preceding the horselitter in which the old man had travelled, was passing beneath the tower. Matauc would need some time to recover and refresh himself, but then Artor would no doubt be wanting her to extend an official welcome. It was time for her to go do so.

Dark and light, shadowed and bright, the oblong of the doorway flickered as the princes of Britannia came into the new henge hall. The flare and glint of gold, abruptly extinguished, dazzled the eye, and Betiver, standing at his accustomed place at Artor's shoulder, had to look away. After a moment his vision adjusted, and he began counting once more.

Light coming in beneath the low eaves where the wicker screens had been removed lent the lower parts of the interior a diffuse illumination, and the fire in the center cast a warm glow; beneath the peak of the roof, all was shadow. Betiver suppressed a smile as he watched the princes and their followers attempting to figure out which were the most honorable benches when the seating was circular. That was exactly why Merlin had suggested that Artor build this round hall. In the end, the choice of seats became roughly geographical, as the little groups found places near their allies and neighbors.

Matauc of Durnovaria had taken a seat beside Leodagranus, just down from Cataur of Dumnonia, who had brought his son Constantine. The Demetian contingent was dominated by Agricola, a war-leader from an old Roman family who made up in effectiveness for what he lacked in bloodlines. Being Roman, he did not call himself a prince, but Protector, though his powers were the same. He had also brought a son, called Vortipor. His northern neighbor was Catwallaun Longhand, still bearing the scars of his last campaign against the Irishmen of Laigin who had settled there under king Illan.

There were other, more familiar faces: old Eleutherius from Eboracum and his son Peretur, Eldaul who ruled the area around Glevum, and Catraut, who kept a wary eye on the Saxons of the east from Verulamium. As his gaze moved around the circle it was the younger men who drew Betiver's attention. They were the ones upon whose strength Artor would build Britannia, whose focus was on the future.

But the silver hairs of age and experience were still much in evidence. Ridarchus had come down from Dun Breatann. He was as old as Leudonus, though he looked stronger. Men said he was married to a sister of Merlin. Betiver found it hard to imagine. Next to him was his half-brother Dumnoval, a grandson of the great Germanianus, who now held the Votadini lands south of the Tava under Leudonus, who had been too ill to come.

Instead, young Cunobelinus was there to speak for the Votadini of Dun Eidyn. There had some discussion about that earlier, for Gualchmai was Leudonus' named heir. But Gualchmai was sitting on Artor's right hand, as Cai held the place on his left, and no one had dared to ask whether that meant the northerner had renounced his birthright to serve the High King, or was claiming a greater one, as Artor's heir.

It seemed unlikely, for although in a year of marriage the queen had not kindled, she was young and healthy, and surely one day she would bear a child. As if the thought had been a summons, Betiver noted a change in the faces of the men across the circle and turned to see Guendivar herself, standing in a nimbus of light in the doorway.

Old or young, men fell silent as the High Queen made her

way around the circle, carrying the great silver krater by the handles at each side. This, thought Betiver, was not the laughing girl who had become his friend, but the High Queen, remote and perfect as an icon in a dalmatic of creamy damask set with pearls, the finest of linen veiling her hair beneath the diadem. As she came to each man, she offered the krater. As the wine flowed over the bright silver, it caught the light with a garnet-colored glow.

"The blood of the grape is the blood of the land," she said softly. "And you are its strong arms. Drink in peace, drink in unity, and be welcome in this hall . . ."

"Lady, you lend us grace—" murmured Vortipor, and then flushed as he realized he had spoken aloud. But no one else seemed to notice—he was saying no more than what they all felt, after all.

Guendivar completed the circle and brought the krater to Artor. "The blood of the grape is the blood of the land, and you, Pendragon, are its head—"

Artor's hands closed over hers on the krater, drawing her closer as he lifted it to his lips. His face bore an expression Betiver had never seen there before—he could not tell if it were joy or pain. Then he let go, looking up at her.

"As you are its heart, my queen . . ." he murmured. For a moment his eyes closed. When he opened them again his features had regained their usual calm. Now it was Guendivar in whose eyes Betiver saw pain. For a moment the queen bowed her head, then she lifted the krater once more and with the same gliding gait bore it out of the hall.

Slowly the murmur of conversation resumed, but the mood had changed. It reminded Betiver of something—abruptly he remembered rapt faces in the church of his boyhood when the icon of the Virgin had been carried around. His breath caught—was the thought sacrilege? A churchman might say so, but his heart told him that a power that was in its way as holy as anything blessed by the church had rested upon the queen as she moved through the hall.

But Artor was speaking—

"In my own name, also, I bid you welcome. We have much to discuss, and more to think on. The Saxons are beaten and for a time their oaths will hold them. We must plan how to use that time to keep them divided in heart and in territory, so that they do not combine against us again. We must plan also a new campaign against the men of Eriu who have seized land in Demetia, and bring it once more under British rule. But these tasks, however pressing, are only a beginning. For too long, force has been our only governor—if we wish to restore the security we knew under the Romans, we must return to the rule of law."

Betiver shifted his weight as Artor's opening speech continued. If he had stayed at home in Gallia, he thought, he might have been addressing such a meeting in his own father's hall. But like Gualchmai, he had chosen to remain in Britannia and serve Artor.

In the afternoon Artor released the members of the council to rest, to think on the matters he had set before them, and to seek exercise. Betiver offered to guide some of the younger men around the countryside, and when he met them at the horse pens, he found that Guendivar, dressed for riding, was waiting too. Her presence might inhibit some of their speech, but she would not impede their exercise. He knew already that she could ride as well as any man. And if the princes were dubious—he smiled quietly—they were in for a surprise.

Certainly the girl who leaped unassisted to the back of the white mare Artor had given her was a very different creature from the image of sovereignty who had brought them wine in the hall. For riding, Guendivar wore breeches and a short tunic. Only the linen cloth that bound her hair showed her to be a woman, and the embroidered blue mantle pinned at the shoulder, a queen.

When they were mounted, it was she who led the way. Indeed, thought Betiver as he brought up the rear, she could have guided the visitors with no help from him. But as he watched her laugh at some word of Peretur's, or smile at young Vortipor, he realized that it was not her safety, but her reputation, he would be guarding today.

At the bottom of the steep hill, Guendivar reined in. They

had departed through the gate on the northeast side of the hill, past the well. From its base, the road ran straight towards the little village that had grown up in the days when the only structure on the hill was the shrine. The queen's mare snorted and shook its head and she laughed.

"Swanwhite wants to stretch her legs!" She gestured towards the village. "Do you think you can catch her if we run?"

By the time they arrived at the village, both horses and riders were quite willing to keep to a more leisurely pace. Guendivar's head wrap had come off and her hair tumbled down her back in a tangle of spilled gold. Her cheeks were flushed, her eyes bright. She looked, thought Betiver, twice as alive as the woman who had stood beside Artor in the council hall, and he felt an odd pang in the region of his heart.

They ambled through the spring green of the countryside, talking. In the warmth of her presence, Vortipor and the other princes lost all their shyness. The air rumbled with their deep laughter. *She is charming them*, thought Betiver. *Artor should be pleased.*

Vortipor told them a long story about hunting stag in the mountains of Demetia, and Peretur countered with a tale of a bear hunt in the dales west of Eboracum. Everyone, it seemed, had some tale of manly prowess—vying with words, the young men strutted and pranced like stallions before a mare. It was Ebicatos, the Irishman who commanded the garrison at Calleva, who protested that the queen must be becoming bored by all these stories of blood and battle, though Betiver had seen no sign of it in her face. But when the Irishman praised her white mare for winning the race to the village, and began the tale of the Children of Lir, who had been transformed by a jealous stepmother into swans, Guendivar listened with parted lips and shining eyes.

Their ride brought them around in a wide half-circle to the southwest. When the hill loomed before them once more, they slowed. The young men gazed at it in amazement. It did not seem possible they had come all this way so quickly, but the sun, which had reached its zenith when they set out, was well along in its downward slide.

The evening session of the council would be beginning. Merlin had returned from his most recent wanderings, and tonight he would report on what he had seen. That should be more interesting than the endless debates they had been listening to, though it would no doubt lead to more.

"Ah, lady," cried Vortipor, "I wish we did not have to return. I wish we could ride westward without stopping until we reached the sea, and then our horses would all become swans, to carry us to the Isles of the Hesperides!"

"The Isles of the Blessed, the Isle of Fair Women, and the Isle of Birds—" murmured Ebicatos.

"There is no need, surely, when the fairest of all women is here with us on this hallowed isle," said Peretur. He caught her outstretched hand and kissed it fervently.

Betiver's breath caught as Guendivar's beauty took on an intensity that was almost painful. Then she shook her head and bitterness muted her radiance like a cloud hiding the sun.

"And here I must stay—" A sudden dig of the heels sent her mare curvetting forward. Startled to silence, the others followed.

What is this that I am feeling? Betiver asked himself as they began to climb the hill. *My sweet Roud is a good woman, and I love her and my son . . .*

The red-headed Alban girl whom he had tumbled in the inebriation of the Feast of Lugus eleven years before had been an unexpected mate, but a good one. It was a soldier's marriage, unblessed by the Church, but recorded by the clerks of Artor's army. But the contentment Roud brought him had nothing in common with the painful way his heart leaped when he looked at Guendivar. A glance at the other men told him that they felt the same. They would serve her—they would die for her—with no hope of any reward beyond a word or a smile.

She is Venus—the remnants of a Classical education prompted him, *and we are her worshippers. And that is only fitting, for she is the queen.* But as they clattered beneath the gatehouse he wondered why, with such a woman in his bed, did the king seem to have so little joy?

*   *   *

Artor is not happy. . . . Merlin glanced at the king from beneath his bushy brows and frowned. Seated on the king's right hand, he could not look at him directly, but the evidence of his eyes only confirmed what other senses had been telling him. Artor was paler than he had been, and thickening around the middle—those changes were a natural result of sitting so much in council chambers and eating well. But there was something haunted about his eyes.

It was not the council, which was going as well as such things ever did. It had become clear that Roman order would never return to Britannia until Roman law ruled once more. The princes must learn to think of themselves as *rectors*, and their war-leaders as *duces*, the generals of the country. Those who had ruled as chieftains had to become judges and magistrates, deriving their power from rector and emperor once more. Thus, and in this way only, could they separate their civilization from the ways of the barbarians.

To Merlin, longing for his northern wilderness, they were both equally constricting, but he had been born to serve the Defender of Britannia, and with him, its Law. Artor's attempts to restore the old ways even looked as if they might be successful. He should have been, if not triumphant, at least well pleased. Something was wrong, and Merlin supposed it was his duty to try and set it right. The thought made him tired, and he yearned to be back in the forest and the undemanding society of the wild folk who lived there. One day, he thought then, he would seek those green mysteries and not return.

The tone of the voices around him changed and he brought his awareness back to the present. The discussion of titles and duties was coming to a close.

"That is well, then, and we can move to the next topic," said Artor. "The Saxons. Merlin has been going among them—they seem to respect him as a holy man—and I believe we can benefit from his observations."

Merlin's lips twitched. He had wandered through the territory of the enemy in times past in safety, protected by their respect for those they thought old or mad. Their response to him now was different, and he knew why.

As if the thought had awakened it, he felt a throb of force from the rune-carved Spear that leaned against his chair, and the familiar pressure in his mind, as if Someone were listening. The head of the Spear was shrouded in silk, and a wrapping of leather thongs hid the runes carved into the shaft, but it still carried the power of the god Woden, and when Merlin came to a Saxon farmstead, holding that staff and with his long beard flying and an old hat drawn down over his eyes, he knew whom they believed him to be.

Merlin got to his feet and moved to the central hearth, leaning on the Spear. Artor straightened, eyes narrowing, as if something within him scented its power. Or perhaps it was the Sword at his side that had recognized another Hallow. Once, the god of the Spear had fought the one that lived in the Sword, but now they seemed to be in alliance. He must explain to Artor what had happened, one day.

But for now, he had to tell these British leaders what he had seen in the Saxon lands.

"In Cantium, the lady Rigana has gathered a council of thanes to advise her. The child, Oesc's son, is healthy, and the men seem very willing to support an extended regency. Many of their young warriors died at Mons Badonicus. They have sufficient men to defend the coasts against small groups of raiders, but I do not believe they will be a danger to us until at least another generation is grown."

"That is all very well," said Catraut, "but what about the Saxons of the south and west?"

"Aelle is an old man—" said Merlin. *My age, but Mons Badonicus broke him. . . .* "He will not ride to war again. And Ceretic's son is little more than a boy. Even if he should seek vengeance, it is clear that his father's thanes will not support him."

"And the Anglians?" asked Peretur.

"There also, for different reasons, I see no danger," said Merlin, and began to lay out his analysis of Icel's position as sacred king, and the reasons why the oath he had given Artor would continue to bind him.

"Separate, these tribes do not present a danger. It is my counsel that you choose brave men to settle the lands that lie between their holdings. So long as the Saxons perceive their portions as tribal territories, they will find it hard to combine. They may hold half Britannia, but they will not see it that way, and so long as you, my lords, remain united, you will be the stronger."

Even Cataur of Dumnonia could see that this was good counsel. Merlin resumed his seat as the princes of Britannia began to debate which borderlands should be resettled, and where they would find the men.

That night, after everyone had eaten, Merlin walked along the sentryway built into the wall, troubled in his mind. While they feasted, he had watched Artor, seated at the central table with his lady beside him. The king should have been smiling, for the council had gone well that day. With a wife like Guendivar, he should have been eager to retire. But though Artor's body showed his awareness of her every movement, they did not touch, and his smiles did not reach his eyes. And when the queen made her farewells and departed into the royal chamber that was partitioned off from the main part of the hall, the king remained talking with Eldaul and Agricola by the fire.

A full moon was rising, its cool light glittering from the open water of pond and stream, and glowing softly in the mist that rose off the fields. The distant hills seemed ghostly; in that glimmering illumination, he could not tell if it was with the eyes of the flesh or of the spirit that he saw, away to the northwest, the pointed shape of the Tor.

Merlin had been standing there for some time, drinking in peace as a thirsty man gulps water, when he sensed that he was no longer alone. A pale shape moved along the walkway, too graceful to be any of the men. The White Phantom that was one meaning of her name . . . Guendivar. . . .

He drew his spirit entirely into his body once more and took a step towards her. She whirled, the indrawn gasp of her breath loud in the stillness, and pressed her back against the wall.

"It is true, you *can* make yourself invisible!"

"Not invisible, only very still. . . . I came to enjoy the peace of the night," he answered, extending his awareness to encompass her, smiling a little as the tension left her body and she took a step towards him.

"So did I . . ." she said in a low voice.

"I thought you would have been in bed by now, with your husband—"

She jerked, staring. "What do you mean? What do you know?"

"I know that all is not well between you. I know that you have no child . . ." he said softly.

She straightened, drawing dignity around her, and he felt her barriers strengthening.

"You have no right—" Her voice shook.

"I am one of the guardians of Britannia, and you are the High Queen. What is wrong, Guendivar?"

"Why do you assume the fault is mine? Ask Artor!"

He shook his head. "The power passes from male to female, and from female to male. You are the Lady of Britannia. If the difficulty is his, still, the healing must come from you."

"And I suppose the knowledge of how to do that will come from *you*? You flatter yourself, old man!" She turned, watching him over her shoulder.

Her hair was silver-gilt in the light of the moon. Even he, who had admitted desire for only one mortal woman in his lifetime, felt a stirring of the senses. But he shook his head.

"The body serves the spirit," he said steadily. "It is in the spirit that I would teach you."

"Tell the woman who wounded Artor to help him! Let him seek healing from the mother of his son! Then, perhaps, he can come to me!"

In the instant that shock held him still she flowed into motion. For a few moments he heard the patter of her retreating footsteps, and then she was gone. Even then, a word of power could have held her, but to such work as he would bid her, the spirit could not be constrained.

Igierne had foreseen this. But she had not seen the mother, only the child. The child would bring war to Britannia, but its mother had already struck a heavy blow. Who was she?

In one thing, Guendivar had the right of it, he thought then. He must speak to Artor.

The fortress had been closed up for the night, but the guard on duty at the north gate was a very young man, and half in love with his queen, so he let her through. *They are all in love with me!* Guendivar thought bitterly. *All except the only one I am allowed to love.*

Stumbling in her haste, she made her way down the trail to the well. A pale shape swooped across the path and she started and nearly fell. For a moment she stared, heart pounding, then relaxed as she saw that it was only a white owl. On such a night, when the sky was clear and the full moon sailed in triumph through the skies, she felt stifled indoors. Even Julia's warm arms were a prison, where she stifled beneath the weight of the other woman's need.

Guendivar had thought a walk on the walls would allow her spirit to soar as freely as the bird, but Merlin was before her. What had she said to him? Surely he, who knew everything, must have known about Artor. The old sorcerer had offered her help—for a moment she wondered if she had been a fool to flee.

But how could a change in *her* do any good? The sin was Artor's, if sin it was—certainly he seemed to think so. He had attempted to be a husband to her two times after that first disastrous encounter, with even less success than on their wedding night. After that, they had not tried again. He was kind to her, and in public gave her all honor, but in the bed that should have been the heart and wellspring of their marriage, they slept without touching, proximity only making them more alone.

Guendivar knew this path well, but she had never been here in the night. In the uncertain light, the familiar shapes of the lower ramparts swelled like serpent coils. Beneath the melancholy calling of the owl she could hear the sweet music of running water. Everywhere else, the trees had been cut to clear a field of fire from the the walls of the fortress, but halfway down the hill, birch trees still clustered protectively around the spring.

Guendivar had never visited the hill until Artor began to build his fortress there, but the people of her father's lands had many tales of the days when it had been a place of pilgrimage. When the lords of Lindinis became Christian they had ceased to support the shrine, and after its last priestess died, the square building with its deep porch had fallen into decay. Now its tumbled stones were part of Artor's walls.

But the sacred spring from which the priestesses had drawn water to use in their spells of healing remained, bubbling up from the depths beneath the hill to form a quiet pool. The stone coping that edged it was worn, but the spout that channeled the overflow had remained clear. From there, it fell in a musical trickle down the hillside in a little stream. Moonlight, filtering through the birch trees, shrouded pool and stone alike in dappled shade.

Guendivar blinked, uncertain, in that glamoured illumination, of her way. The old powers had been banished from the hilltop, but here she could still feel them. She stretched out her arms, calling as she had called when she ranged the hills at home. Gown and mantle weighted her limbs; she stripped them off and unpinned the heavy coils of her hair. She stretched, exulting in the free play of muscle and limb. A little breeze lifted the fine strands and caressed her naked body, set the birch leaves shivering until the shifting dappling of moonlight glittered on the troubled waters of the pool.

Light swirled above it like a mist off the waters, shaping the form of a woman, clad, like Guendivar, only in her shining hair.

"Who are you?" Guendivar whispered. She was accustomed to the folk of faerie, but this was a being of nobler kind than any she had met before.

"I am Cama, the curve of the hill and the winding water, I am the sacred round. It has been long . . . very long . . . since any mortal called to Me. . . . What is your need?"

Guendivar felt her skin pebble with holy fear. The new faith had not yet succeeded in banishing the old wisdom so completely that she could not recognize the ancient goddess of this part of the land. But her cry had been wordless. She struggled for an answer.

"The water flows—the wind blows—but I am bound! I want to be free!"

"*Free . . .*" The goddess tested the sound as if she did not quite understand. "*The waters flow downhill to the sea . . . heat and cold drive the currents of the wind. They are free to follow their natures. Is that what you desire?*"

"And what is my nature? I am wed, but no wife!"

"*You are the Queen . . .*"

"I am a gilded image. I have no power—"

"*You* are *the power . . .*"

Guendivar, her mouth still opening in protest, halted, almost understanding. Then the owl called, and the insight was gone. She saw the figure of the Lady dislimning into a column of glimmering light.

"Help me!" she cried. She heard no answer, but the figure opened its arms.

Shivering, Guendivar climbed over the coping and stepped into the pool. Soft mud gave beneath her feet and she slid into the cold depths too swiftly for a scream. Water closed over her head, darkness enclosed her. *This is death*, she thought, but there was no time for fear. And then she was rushing upwards into the light. Power swirled around her, but she was the center of the circle—*being* and *doing*, the motion and her stillness, one and the same.

In this place there was no time, but time must have passed, for presently, with no sense of transition, Guendivar found herself experiencing the world with her normal senses once more. The moon had moved a quarter of the way across the sky, and its light no longer fell full on the pool. She was standing, streaming with water, but the bottom of the pool was solid beneath her feet.

She felt empty, and realized that what had departed from her was her despair. Perhaps this serenity would not last, but she did not think she would ever entirely forget what she had seen.

THE WOUNDED KING

A·D· 498

GUENDIVAR HUDDLED NEXT TO THE HEARTH OF THE HOUSE the king's household had commandeered, listening to the hiss of the fire and the dull thud of rain on the thatching. If she sat any closer, she thought unhappily, she would catch fire herself, but her back still felt damp even when her front was steaming.

None of the other dwellings in this village were any better. She pitied the men of Artor's army, shivering in the dubious shelter of tents made of oiled hide as they cursed the Irish. The euphoria of their great victory at Urbs Legionis—the city of legions that was also called Deva—had worn away. Illan, king of the men of Laigin who had settled in northern Guenet a generation ago, was on the run, but he was going to make the British fight for every measure of ground between Deva and the Irish Sea.

She laid another stick on the fire, wondering why she had been so eager to accompany Artor on this campaign. For most of the past week it had been raining, grey veils of cloud dissolving into the silver sea. With each day's march, the stony hills that edged the green pasturelands had grown nearer. Now they rose in a grim wall on the left, broken by an occasional steep glen from which shrieking bands of Irishmen might at any moment emerge to harry the army that was pushing steadily westward along the narrowing band of flat land between the mountains and the sea.

Artor was up ahead somewhere with the scouts. It had been foolish to think that their relationship might improve if she accompanied him. The king spent his days in the saddle, returning tired, wet, and hungry when night fell, usually escorting wounded men. Artor had not wanted to bring her, but during their brief courtship he had said she could ride with the army, and she had sworn she would neither complain nor slow them down.

There was no risk of the latter, Guendivar thought bitterly, since she travelled with the rearguard. As for complaining, so far she had held her tongue, but she knew that if she had to stay cooped up in this hut for much longer she was going to scream.

With that thought, she found that she was on her feet and turning towards the door. She pushed past the cowhide that covered it and stood beneath the overhang of the roof, breathing deeply of the clean air. It was damp, heavy with mingled scents of wet grass and seaweed. Mist still clung to the hilltops, but a fresh wind was blowing, and here and there a stray gleam of sunlight spangled the sea.

It might only be temporary, but the skies were clearing. Guendivar gazed longingly at the slopes whose green grew brighter with every moment. Surely, she told herself, they could not be entirely different from the gentle hills of her home. Some of the same herbs would grow there, plants that her old nurse had taught her to use in healing. . . .

The young soldier who had been assigned to her personal escort straightened as she came out into the open. His name was Cau, one of the men who had come down from the Votadini lands with Marianus. There was some tension between the followers of Marianus and Catwallaun, both grandsons of the great Cuneta, though Catwallaun's branch of the family had been settled in Guenet a generation before. Many of the newcomers resented being set to guard the rear of the army, but Cau had attached himself to Guendivar's service with a dedication reminiscent of those monks who served the Virgin Mary. He had left a wife back in Deva with their infant son, Gildas, but he still flushed crimson whenever Guendivar smiled.

"Look—it has stopped raining." She stretched out a hand, palm upward, and laughed. "We should take advantage of the change in weather. I would ride a little way into those hills to gather herbs for healing."

Cau was already shaking his head. "My lord king ordered me to keep you safe here—"

"The king has also ordered that his wounded be cared for. Surely he would not object if I go out in search of medicines to help them. Please, Cau—" she gave him a tremulous smile "—I think I will go mad if I do not get some exercise. Surely all the enemy are far ahead of us by now!"

Cau still looked uncertain, but he and his men were as frustrated by their inaction as she was. She suppressed a smile, knowing even before he spoke that he was going to agree.

After the stink and smoke of the hut, to be out in the fresh air was heaven. When the grasslands began to slope upward, they dismounted, and Guendivar wandered over the meadow searching for useful herbs while Cau followed with a basket and the other men sat their horses, grinning in their beards.

Guendivar made sure she found enough herbs among the grasses to justify the expedition. She picked the five-lobed leaves of Lady's Mantle and Self-heal with its clustered purple trumpets, both good for cleansing wounds. As they wandered farther, she glimpsed the creamy flowers and tooth-shaped leaves of Traveller's Joy, whose bark made an effective infusion for reducing fever, and Centaury, also good for fever, and for soothing the stomach and toning the system as well. Purging Flax went into the basket, and wild Marjoram to bathe sore muscles and reduce bruises.

It was a hard land, whipped by the sea winds, and nowhere did the useful plants grow in abundance, but by midafternoon they had nearly filled the basket. Her men had earned a rest, and Guendivar led them towards the musical trickle of water that came from a small ravine. The stream itself was hidden by a fringe of hazel and thorn, with a few straggling birch trees, but after all the running about she had been doing, its moist breath was welcome.

She had opened her mouth to tell Cau to bring the bread and cheese from her saddlebags when a wild shriek and a crashing in the bushes brought her whirling around. From out of the brush men came leaping, brandishing spears. There must have been fifty of them, against the dozen men of the queen's guard. Her escort spurred their mounts forward to meet them, but the ground was steep and broken; two horses went down and the others plunged as men ran towards them.

"Selenn! Run! Get help—" cried Cau. The last of the riders pulled up as the attackers surrounded the others, stabbing with their spears. In another moment he had hauled his mount's head around and was galloping down the slope.

Cau grabbed Guendivar's arm and thrust her down, standing over her with drawn sword. One enemy got too close and a sweeping swordstroke felled him, but a word from the leader directed the others towards the rest of her escort, and in minutes they were dead or captive, and the queen and her protector surrounded by leveled spears. Guendivar got to her feet, chin held up defiantly.

"You will be putting down your blade now, and none will harm you—" said the leader. An Irish accent, of course—but she had guessed that from the jackets and breeches of padded leather they wore.

"Artor will kill me . . ." muttered Cau, lowering his sword.

Guendivar shook her head. "It was my will, my responsibility—"

The enemy leader made a swift step forward, took the weapon and handed it to one of his men. He drew two lengths of thong from his belt and tied first Cau's and then Guendivar's hands.

"Come now, for we have far to go."

"You are mad," said the queen. "Release us, and perhaps Artor will not hunt you down."

"Lady, would you be refusing our hospitality?" He eyed her appreciatively. "I'm thinking that your king will pay well to have you back again."

One of the spears swung purposefully towards Cau's back. The warrior's grin told her he would not hesitate to spear his captive, and Guendivar started forward, knowing that Cau must follow her.

"It is myself, Melguas son of Ciaran, that has the honor to be your captor," he said over his shoulder, teeth flashing in his russet beard. His hair was more blond than red, confined in many small braids bound and ornamented with bits of silver and gold. He led the way at a swift trot and it took all Guendivar's breath to keep up with him.

"It is Guendivar daughter of Leodagranus who has the misfortune to be your captive, and lord Cau, who commands my guards," she said when they paused for a moment at the top of the slope. The ravine deepened here, and in the shelter of the trees ponies were waiting, surefooted native beasts that could go swiftly on the rough terrain.

"And do you think we did not know it? For many and many a day we have been watching you." Melguas tipped back his head, laughing, and she saw the torque of silver that gleamed beneath the beard.

"A damned cheerful villain," murmured Cau, but Guendivar closed her eyes in pain. This had been no evil chance, but the enemy's careful plan, waiting only on her foolishness. She thought of the three men of her escort whom the Irish had left dead on the field and knew their blood was on her hands.

Darkness had fallen by the time they stopped at last, and they had covered many miles. Sick at heart and aching from the pony's jolting, Guendivar allowed Melguas to pull her off the horse and thrust her into a brush hut without protest. They left Cau to lie beside the fire, still bound, with a blanket thrown over him. It did no good to tell herself that Artor would be as wounded by the loss of any of his companions as by her capture—none of *them* could have been taken so easily.

That night she huddled in the odorous blankets in silent misery. How long, she wondered, before Selenn reached the rearguard and told his tale? How long for another messenger to get to Artor? By the time he could send men to her rescue, the rain she heard pattering on the brush would have wiped out their trail. *Perhaps he will think himself well rid of me. . . .* She contemplated the prospect of an endless captivity with sour satisfaction. She was glad now that Julia had been left behind in Camalot, so that she was not weighted by the burden of the sister's grief as well.

In the morning she was given a bowl of gruel and made to mount the pony once more. For most of the day they moved steadily, following the hidden paths through the hills. Here in the high country, the wind blew cold and pure, as if it had never passed through mortal lungs; an eagle, hanging in the air halfway between the earth and the sun, was the only living thing they saw. When Guendivar expressed surprise that the Irish should know these paths, Melguas laughed.

"My father is a prince in the land of Laigin, but 'tis here I was born and I am on speaking terms with every peak and valley."

As I am in the Summer Country, Guendivar thought then, wishing she were there now. "Are you taking me to King Illan?" she asked aloud.

"Surely—better than a wall of stone to protect us is the lovely body of Artor's queen."

"Do not be so certain," Guendivar said grimly.

"How not?" Melguas looked at her in surprise. "Are you not the White Lady, with the fertility of the land between your round thighs and its sovereignty shining from your brow?"

Not for Artor, thought Guendivar, but she would not betray him by saying so. These Irish seemed so confident of her value—what magic did queens have, there in Eriu, that these exiled sons should hold them in such reverence? Melguas had forced her obedience, but neither he nor his men had dared to offer her either insult or familiarity. *This is what Merlin was trying to tell me,* she thought then, *but I must be a fraud as well as a failure, for there is something missing within me that prevents me from becoming truly Artor's queen!*

* * *

That night they slept wrapped in cloaks beneath rude brush shelters. In the middle of the night, Guendivar felt the need to relieve herself and crawled out from the shelter, shivering as the chill touched her skin. The privy trench had been dug a little down the slope. When she was finished, she stood, gazing at the black shapes of the mountains humped against the stars. If this had been her own country, she would have tried to slip away in the darkness, but she did not know this land, and besides, Melguas was a careful commander, and though she could not see them, there would be guards.

She turned, and as if the thought had summoned him, saw a dark man-shape rising out of the rocks.

"Ah, lady, you are cold—let me make you warm—"

It was Melguas, but something within her had already known it. With a sense of inevitability, she felt his hands close on her shoulders, the scent of male sweat as he pulled her against him and kissed her mouth.

"I am a queen—" she whispered when he released her at last. "Is this how you respect me?" But her heart was thumping in her breast, and she had not wanted him to let her go.

"It is—as I would serve the land herself, had she a body I could worship . . ." The soft Irish voice was trembling, but his grip was firm.

I must stop this, Guendivar told herself as he pulled her close once more, his hands reverent on her skin. But if she cried out, no one would help her—there would only be more witnesses to her shame. His hand moved to her breast, and she swayed, all her frustrated sensuality asserting its claim. He laughed then, sensing her body yielding, and bore her to the shelter of a stony outcrop and on the soft grass laid her down.

Pressed against the earth by the weight of Melguas' body, the queen had no power of resistance. And at the moment of fulfillment, it seemed to her as if she *was* the earth, opening ecstatically to receive his love.

Guendivar woke, shamed and aching, to a soft drizzle that continued throughout the day. She drew her shawl over her head, peering at the faces of the warriors. But there were no sly looks or secret smiles, and if Melguas looked triumphant, her capture was excuse enough. Perhaps her secret was secure. She wondered if Cau suspected. Their captors had left him bound all night, and he must be feeling even worse than she was. He sat his pony without complaining, but he no longer smiled.

The cloud cover was beginning to darken when Melguas drew rein.

"Illan's camp lies yonder—" He gestured towards the next fold in the hills, and it seemed to Guendivar, accustomed after two days to the cold silences of the heights, that she could hear a distant murmur like a river in flood. "If you wish it, we will be stopping for a moment so that you may dress your hair and brush your garments and appear before my lord as a queen." There was a familiar warmth in his gaze.

Guendivar stared at him. Riding with Artor's men, she had packed away her royal ornaments so that they would think of her as a sister and comrade. After two days in the saddle, she must look like one of the women who followed the army, her face grimed and bits of brush tangled in her hair. *If all my jewels cannot make me a real queen, how will it serve if I tidy my hair?*

Melguas was waiting. Guendivar's mother had been constantly carping at her to at least *pretend* she was a lady. Why should this be any different? For three years now she had been pretending to be a queen. What had happened to her last night should have destroyed even the pretense of legitimacy, but her captor's belief compelled her. She took the comb the Irishman held out to her and began to untangle her braids.

Through the veil of her hair she could see the light in Melguas' eyes become a flame of adoration. As the red-gold strands blew out upon the wind the other men stared, even Cau had straightened in the saddle, watching with some of his old worship in his eyes. Their faces were mirrors in which she saw the reflection of a queen. She slowed, drawing out each stroke of the comb with intention, drawing from the men who watched her the power to become what they needed her to be.

And in that moment, when the attention of her captors was focused on her beauty, riders burst suddenly over the rim of the hill and the warcry of the Pendragon echoed against the sky.

Gualchmai was in the lead, as big and barbaric as any of the Irishmen. Melguas made a grab for Guendivar's rein, but she recovered from the first shock of recognition in time to boot her pony into motion. She dropped the comb and grabbed for its mane as the beast leaped into a jolting canter, managing to collect the reins herself in time to stop the animal before it ran away with her.

By this time Melguas and Gualchmai were trading blows, the clangor of steel assaulting the trembling air. She glimpsed Betiver and Cai and Gualchmai's brothers—Christ! Artor had sent all his Companions! And then she realized that he had not sent but led them, that the big man in silver mail and the spangenhelm that hid his features was Artor himself, charging into battle like the Great Bear.

She had never before seen Artor in combat. Gualchmai fought with more gleeful ferocity, Betiver with more precision, but Artor faced his foes with a grim intensity she had not observed in any other man, the Chalybe blade falling like the stroke of doom on any fighter who dared to face him.

Is this for me, wondered Guendivar, *or for his honor? Or for the sake of that imaginary being, the High Queen?*

Just as the Irishmen had overmatched her escort, they were overwhelmed by Artor's Companions, even though they outnumbered them. In a few moments, it seemed, her captors were dead or fleeing, except for Melguas himself, who was still holding off Betiver and Aggarban, laughing. But they fell back when Artor finished off his last opponent and strode towards them, his bloody sword poised.

"Not worthy of her—" Melguas said breathlessly, "but I see . . . you are an honorable man!"

Silently, Artor settled into a fighter's crouch, every line in his body expressing deadly purpose. Melguas' eyes narrowed, as if he had only now begun to appreciate the caliber of his enemy, and he braced his feet, lifting his sword. For a long moment, neither man stirred. Then, as if at some unspoken signal, both fighters blurred into action. The swords moved too swiftly for her eye to follow, but when the two figures separated, Artor was still upright, and Melguas was falling, a red gash opening like a flower across his belly and breast.

Guendivar let out a breath she had not known she was holding in a long sigh. Melguas lay where he had fallen, chest heaving in loud gasps as blood spread over his leather armor and began to drip onto the ground. She took a step forward, and then another, staring in appalled fascination at the wreck of the man who had made her captive.

"End it—" whispered Melguas. "You . . . have the best of me. . . ."

"My lord," Betiver started forward, dagger already drawn, "there is no need for you to soil your hands—"

Artor shook his head. "A good hunter always finishes off his kill." He took the dagger from Betiver and knelt beside his foe, laying his sword beside him on the ground.

Melguas twisted, his body contorting as if momentarily overcome by pain. Only Guendivar, coming closer, saw his fingers close on the hilt of the dagger strapped to his thigh. In the moment it took her mind to comprehend what her eyes had seen, Melguas jerked the weapon free and slashed upward beneath the hanging skirt of Artor's mail.

The king jerked away with a muffled oath.

"No good to her—" Melguas began, but Artor, his face suffused with fury, reeled forward, supporting himself on his left hand, and with his right plunged the dagger into his enemy's throat above the silver torque and tore sideways so that the Irishman's head flopped suddenly to the side, his eyes still widening in surprise.

Artor stared down at him, grimacing, then slowly collapsed to his side, blood spreading down the cloth of his breeches.

"Artor!" "My lord!" Gualchmai and Betiver cried out together as they reached his side. Carefully they stretched him out, dragging the mail aside. The dagger had torn the flesh of Artor's inner thigh and all the way up into the groin. The king made no sound, but his skin was paling, and his body quivered with the pain.

"He didn't get the artery—" murmured Betiver, peeling the cloth back from the wound. Blood was flowing steadily, but not in the red tide that no surgery could stop.

"Nor yet your manhood!" added Gualchmai, gripping Artor's shoulder. "Let it bleed for the moment—it will clean the wound. Do you lie now on your right side, and we'll get you out of this mail."

Guendivar's fists were clenched in her skirts, but these men knew more of wounds and armor than she. There was nothing she could do until they had got off sword belt and mail shirt and cut away his breeches and were looking for cloth with which to stanch the wound.

After three days in the saddle, her own clothes were none too clean, but she had more, and softer, fabric about her than anything the Companions had to offer. She hauled up her skirts and cut half the front of her shift away, folding it into a pad which she bound across the wound with her veil.

"You will have to make a litter," she told the men. "He cannot ride this way."

"Aye, and swiftly," agreed Gualchmai, "before the bastards that got away are bringing Illan down on us to finish the job."

"Betiver . . . you will lead the army—" whispered Artor as the men began to hack at a young oak tree that clung to the side of the hill. "Take most of the men and head straight for the coast. Pursuit should . . . follow you."

"And what of you, my lord?" Betiver kept his voice steady, but his face was nearly as pale as Artor's own.

"Gualchmai will take . . . me to the Lake . . . to Igierne."

"I will go with you," Guendivar said firmly. Artor, who had not met her gaze since she bandaged his wound, said nothing, and as she stared down the others, she realized that at least for this moment, she was queen in truth as well as name.

When her women came to tell her that a messenger had arrived, Morgause was not surprised—galloping hooves had haunted her dreams. The rider was the man she had sent to be her eyes and ears in Artor's army. As she recognized him, she felt something twist painfully in her belly, and that did surprise her.

"What is it?" she asked, controlling her voice. "Has something happened to the king?"

"He is not dead, my lady," the man said quickly. "But he is wounded, too badly to continue the campaign. He has left Betiver in command."

"Not Gualchmai?" Morgause frowned.

"Your son is with Artor. They are progressing by slow stages northward—no one would say where or why."

"To the Lake—" Morgause said thoughtfully, "that has to be their destination. His wound must be serious indeed, if he goes to my mother for healing."

To Igierne, and to the Cauldron, she added silently, fists clenching in the skirts of her gown. Was the injury so severe, or had Artor seized the excuse to gain access to the Cauldron's mysteries?

"What is the nature of the wound?" she asked then.

"I do not know for certain," said the spy. "He is not able to ride. They say—" he added in some embarrassment "—that the king is wounded in the thighs . . ."

Morgause stifled a triumphant smile. The queen had borne Artor no child. Whether that was because the words she gave to each of them at their wedding had cursed their bed, or it was the will of the gods, she did not know. But if the king was injured in his manhood, it might be long before he could try again to beget an heir. Gualchmai was known to everyone as Artor's sister-son, the bravest of his Companions. Britannia would find it easy to accept him as the king's heir. And if he refused the honor, she still had Medraut. . . .

"You did well to bring me this news." Morgause paused, considering the messenger. He was called Doli, a man of the ancient race of the hills. In feature he was fine-boned and dark, devoted to her service by rites of the old magic. Some years earlier she had arranged for his sister to enter the community of priestesses on the Isle of Maidens.

"Now I have another task for you," she said then. "I wish you to ride to the Lake and pay a visit to your sister. If, as you say, the king's party is moving slowly, you may be there and gone before ever he arrives."

"And when I am come?" Doli lifted one dark eyebrow inquiringly.

"You will give her the flask I shall send with you, and a message. But this, I dare not commit to writing. I shall record it in your memory, and only when your sister Ia speaks the words, 'by star and stone' shall the message be set free.

"It is well—" Doli bowed his head in submission, then settled himself cross-legged on the floor, eyes closed and chest rising and falling in the ancient rhythm of trance.

When she sensed that his energy had sunk and steadied, Morgause called his spirit to attention by uttering his secret name. Then she began to chant the message that he must carry.

"Thus, the words of the Lady of Dun Eidyn who is called the Vor-Tigerna, the Great Queen, to Ia daughter of Malcuin. The priestesses will work the rite of healing for King Artor. Add the contents of the flask your brother shall give you to the water in the pool. When you do this, these are the words you must say: 'Thou art a stagnant pool in a poisoned land, a barren field and a fruitless tree. Thy seed shall fail, and thy sovereignty pass away. By the will of the Great Queen, so shall it be!' "

Morgause waited a moment, then spoke the ritual words to rouse Doli from his trance. Then she sent him off to be fed, and went herself to the hut where she prepared her herbs and brewed her medicines to distill a potion strong enough to counter the power of the Cauldron and all her mother's magic as well.

Asleep, Artor was so like Uthir that Igierne felt the pain of it in her breast each time she looked at him. Perhaps it was because he was ill, and the image of how her husband had appeared in his last years was still vivid in Igierne's memory. But Artor was only thirty-four, and she would not let him die. Even asleep his face showed the lines that responsibility had graven around his mouth and between his brows, and there were more strands of silver in the brown hair.

They had put the king to bed in the guest chamber of the Isle of Maidens, where a fresh breeze off the lake could blow through the window, bearing with it the scent the sun released from the pines. From time to time Artor twitched, as if even in sleep his wound pained him. The Irishman's blade had sliced through the muscles of the inner thigh and up into the groin, but it had not, quite, penetrated the belly. Nor had it cut into his scrotum, although the slash came perilously close. The great danger now was wound fever, for the rough field dressing had done little more than stop the bleeding, and during the jolting journey north the wound had become inflamed.

She leaned forward to stroke the damp hair off of his brow and felt the heat of fever, though it seemed to her that the strong infusion of willow-bark tea she had given Artor when he arrived had begun to bring the burning down. When he was a little rested, they would have to cleanse the wound and pack it with a poultice of spear-leek to combat the infection. As if in anticipation of the pain, Artor twisted restlessly, muttering, and she bent closer to hear.

"Guendivar . . . so beautiful. . . ." That he should call his wife's name was to be expected, but why was there such anguish in his tone? "Did he touch her? Did he . . . I have no right! It was my sin. . . ."

Frowning, Igierne dipped the cloth into the basin of cool water and laid it once more on his brow. She knew that Artor had been wounded by the Irishman who abducted the queen, but Guendivar swore she had not been harmed. Why was he babbling about sin?

"Be easy, my child . . ." she murmured. "It is all over now and you are safe here. . . ."

He shook his head, groaning, as if even in his delirium his mother's words had reached him. "She told me . . . I have a son. . . ."

Igierne sat back, eyes widening. "Who, Artor?" her voice hardened. "Whose son?"

"Morgause . . ." came the answer. "Why should she hate me? I didn't know. . . ."

"It is all right . . . the sin was not yours . . ." Igierne replied, but her mind was racing, remembering a sullen, red-headed boy sorting pebbles on a garden path. She had assumed the family resemblance came all from Morgause—but what if Medraut had a double heritage?

It was no wonder that Artor was fevered, if this knowledge was festering in his memory. It would not be enough to deal with the wound to his body—somehow, she would have to heal his soul.

The Lake was very beautiful, thought Guendivar, especially now, when the first turning leaves of autumn set glimmering reflections of gold and russet dancing in the water, and the tawny hills lifted bare shoulders against a sky that shone pure clear blue after the past days of rain. But after a week cooped up on the island with the priestesses, she felt as confined as she had with the army, and Gualchmai, who was camped with the other men in the meadow by the landing across from the island, had said he would be happy to escort her on a walk along the shore.

"If we are attacked," she said bitterly, "let them take me. I am not worth the lives of any more good men." Throughout that long ride northward, no one had accused her, no one suspected that she had lain in Melguas' arms. In the stress of the journey she had almost been able to forget it herself. But now, with nothing to do, the memory tormented her.

"Lady! You must not say it. You are the queen!" Gualchmai's voice held real pain.

She shook her head. "Igierne is the queen. On the way north Artor needed me, but I have neither the knowledge nor the magic to help him now."

"Nor do I, Guendivar—I would give my heart's blood if it would heal him, but I have no skill to fight the enemy he battles." Gualchmai's broad shoulders slumped.

Hearing the anguish in his voice, the queen found her own a little eased. She breathed in the spicy scent of fallen leaves and exhaled again in a long sigh, feeling tension go out of her. Leaves rustled with each footstep, and squirrels chittered to each other from the trees.

"But you fight his other foes," she said presently. "You are the bulwark of his throne."

"That is all I desire. I am happier on the field of battle than in the council hall. To deal with the bickering of the princes would drive me to blows within a year and plunge the land into civil war."

His tone had brightened, and Guendivar laughed.

"Surely the Lady of the Lake will make the king well again, and I will be spared the temptation," he said then. "She is a wise woman. And she has agreed to take my daughter as one of her maidens here."

"Your daughter! I did not know you had a child," exclaimed Guendivar.

"Until last year, I did not know it either," Gualchmai answered ruefully. "I got her on a woman of the little dark folk of the hills, one time I was out hunting and my pony went lame when I was yet far from home. She is as wild as a doe, but her hair is the same color as my own, and her mother died this past winter, so I must find her a home."

"What is she called?" asked the queen, finding it as hard to imagine Gualchmai a father as he did himself.

"Ninive—"

So Morgause is a grandmother! Does she know? wondered Guendivar, but she did not voice that thought aloud.

"Igierne will understand how to tame her," said Gualchmai. He stooped to pick up a spray of chestnuts brought down by the wind, and stripped off the prickly rind and the leathery shell before offering one to the queen. The nut inside was moist and sweet. "And she will make Artor well."

"She will," Guendivar echoed his affirmation. "His fever has been down for two days now, and they tell me that the wound is beginning to heal."

No man had ever entered the cave of the Cauldron, but in the dell below it, a basin had been hollowed out of the stone foundations of the island which could be filled with water for baths of purification or healing, and here, when there was great need, a man could come. It was large enough for several women to sit together or for a grown man to lie. Here, at dusk when the new moon was first visible in the evening sky, they brought Artor to complete his healing.

The Lady of the Lake sat on a bench at the head of the pool. It was set into the niche where the image of the Goddess had stood since the first priestesses came to the island. Or perhaps before—the image was fashioned from lead, bare-breasted above a bell-shaped skirt, in a style that had been ancient when the Romans came. A terra-cotta lamp cast a wavering light on the image. To Igierne, it seemed that She was smiling.

It would take many weeks before the king was entirely whole, but the wound had closed. For health to return, the balance of his body must be restored, and his bruised spirit persuaded to add its blessing. More lamps flickered around the pool, and the breeze from the lake brought with it the scent of woodsmoke from the fire where they were heating the water. Sometimes she longed for the natural hot springs of Aquae Sulis, and yet there was a more focused magic in the building of a fire and the brewing of the herbs that infused the water.

As the season turned towards autumn the nights were growing cold, but now, while the memory of the sun still glowed in the western sky, the air held the warmth of the afternoon. In the purple dusk the maiden moon hung like a rind of pearl. The air had the hush that comes with the end of day, but as Igierne listened, she began to perceive another sound. Her priestesses were singing as they escorted Artor along the path.

> "Water of life, water of love—
> We come from the Mother and to Her we return..."

Igierne got to her feet. As she raised her arms in welcome, the black folds of her sleeves fell back from her white arms. The silver-and-moonstone diadem of the high priestess was a familiar weight upon her brow.

> "Water of healing flows from above,
> We come from the Mother...."

Two by two, the white-clad priestesses passed between the twin oak trees that guarded the pool, each carrying a vessel of water that steamed gently in the cooling air. The pairs separated to either side, kneeling to pour the contents of the basins into the bath, then rising and turning away to either side to return for more.

"Water of passage, water of birth . . ." the priestesses sang.

As the level of liquid grew, the scents of the herbs that had been steeped in it grew heavy in the air—various mints and camomile, rosemary and lavender, salvia and sweet woodruff and substances such as sea salt and powdered white willow that had little fragrance but great power.

Some of them they grew on the island, and some they gathered in the wild lands, and some were brought from afar. The fragrance was almost dizzying in its intensity. And yet, as Igierne breathed in, something seemed different from before, a hint of something spoiled. She took another breath, testing the air, but it was no scent she recognized. She wondered if it were physical at all, or if she was sensing some spiritual corruption. At the thought, her hands moved instinctively in the gesture used to ward and banish, and her awareness of the wrongness began to pass away.

"Water of blessing flows from the earth . . ."

She shook her head—perhaps it had been her imagination. She knew that with age her senses had become less dependable.

Now the bath was three-quarters full. Nest and Ceincair were coming through the gateway with Artor, wrapped in a green robe between them. He moved slowly, depending on the priestesses for support, but he was on his feet, though the beads of sweat stood out on his brow.

"We come from the Mother and to Her we return . . ." the women sang, and then were still.

The king and his escorts stopped at the edge of the pool.

"Child of the Goddess, why have you come here?" asked Igierne.

"I seek to be healed in body and in soul—" came Artor's answer. She held his gaze, hoping that it was true, for she had not been able to get from him, waking, an explanation of the words he had muttered in his fevered dream.

"Return, then, to the womb of the Mother, and be made whole."

The priestesses untied the cord and eased the robe from his shoulders. Face and arms were sallow where illness had faded his tan, but the rest of Artor's body was pale, growing rosy now as he realized he stood naked before nine women. But their gaze was impersonal, half tranced already by the ritual, and after a moment he regained his composure and allowed Nest and Ceincair to steady him as he descended the steps into the pool.

He halted again at the first level, as if surprised by the heat, then, biting his lip, continued downward until he stood in water halfway up his thighs, the mark of his injury livid against the pale skin. At the end of the bath there was a stone headrest. When the priestesses had helped him all the way down, the headrest enabled him to lie half-floating, his body completely submerged.

The priestesses had settled themselves cross-legged around the pool, singing softly to invoke the healing powers of the herbs. From time to time one of them would fetch more water to maintain the heat of the bath. Gradually the tension faded from Artor's body. He lay with eyes closed, perspiration streaming from his face.

The singing continued as the night grew darker, gradually increasing in intensity. Igierne, who had been watching the gateway, saw first the pale figure appear within it, and then, as if some change in the air had aroused him, a sudden tension in the slack body of the king. He opened his eyes, and they widened as a light that transcended the blaze of the torches glowed around the shining robes of the priestess and the silver Cauldron in her arms.

The wonder remained as the maiden came fully into the light and he saw her dark hair, but the hope that had been there also was gone. Igierne understood. She had tried to persuade Guendivar to bear the Cauldron, and could not understand why the queen would not agree. Neither her son nor her daughter-in-law would share their secrets, but she understood now that Artor loved his queen. For a moment sorrow shook Igierne's concentration. Then the momentum of the ritual swept all other awareness away.

"Be reborn from the water of life!" her voice rang against the stones. "Be healed by the water of love!"

The priestess lifted the cauldron, and the hallowed water it held poured in a stream of light into the pool.

†HE GREA† QUEEⁿ

A·D· 500

†HE SKIRLING OF BAGPIPES THROBBED LIKE AN OLD WOUND IN the chill spring air, so constant that one forgot it until a touch, or a memory, brought the pain of loss to consciousness once more. King Leudonus was dead, and the Votadini were gathering to mourn him. The great dun on the rock of Eidyn was filled with chieftains, and the gorge below crammed with the skin tents and brushwood bothies of their followers. Morgause, marshalling provisions and cooks for the funeral feast, settling quarrels over precedence and ordering the rituals, was too busy to question whether what she felt was grief, or relief that he was gone.

These past ten years she had been a nurse to him, not a wife, watching his strength fade until he lay like a ruined fortress, never leaving his bed. And as the rule of the Votadini had passed into her hands, Morgause had become not only the symbol of sovereignty, but its reality. In his day, Leudonus had been a mighty warrior, but in the end death had taken him from ambush, with no struggle at all. She had drawn aside the curtain that screened his bed place one morning and found him stiff and cold.

It was just as well, thought Morgause as Dumnoval and the

southern Votadini chieftains came marching in, that grief did not overwhelm her, for upon the strength she showed now, her future here would depend. She had sent word to her sons who were with Artor, but she had little hope they would come. The spring campaign against those Irish who still clung to the coasts of Guenet and Demetia had just begun, and the king's nephews were among his most valued commanders.

Perhaps it was as well, for the fighting provided a credible excuse for Gualchmai's absence. As it was, she could pretend that only a greater duty kept him away, though it had long been clear to her just how little he cared for the lordship of his father's land. Nonetheless, just as her marriage to Leudonus had legitimated her authority, her status as mother to the heir might continue to do so, even when everyone knew his rule to be a fiction.

It was not, she thought as she offered the meadhorn to Dumnoval in welcome, as if she had not prepared for this day. There was scarcely a family in the land that had not cause to be grateful for food in a hard year, the loan of a bride-price to win a family alliance, gifts of weapons or cattle or honors. And so, as Dumnoval slid down off his pony, she greeted him as the Great Queen of Alba, receiving one of her men.

That evening she dressed in silk, its crimson folds glowing blood-red in the torchlight. Ornaments of amber and jet gleamed from her neck and wrists, amber drops swung from her ears. For some years now she had used henna to hide the silver in her hair, and kohl to emphasize her eyes. In the firelight, the marks that time and power had graven in her face were hidden. She was forever young, and beautiful. She passed among the benches, smiling, flattering, reminding them of her ties with the Picts and the benefits that a united Alba could bring, persuading them that they still needed her to be their queen.

The next morning, veiled, she walked behind Leudonus' bier, her son Goriat, who at seventeen towered like a young tree, on one side, and the thirteen-year-old Medraut, with his shining bronze hair and secret smile, on the other. Up from the Rock of Eidyn to the Watch Hill above it wound the procession, and then around the slope to the little lake on whose shores they had prepared the pyre. The ashes would be buried by the tribal kingstone below the ancient Votadini fortress, a day's journey to the southeast. It was here where the king had ruled that the Druids chanted their prayers and spells; and here, while the pipes wailed and the drums pounded heavy as heartbeats, that the holy fire released Leudonus' spirit to the winds.

That night the men drank to their dead king's memory while the bards chanted his deeds. The queen remained in the women's quarters, as was fitting. Morgause was grateful for the custom, for her woman's courses, which for several moons had been absent, had returned in a flood. She was lying in her bed, listening to the distant sounds of revelry and wondering whether she could sleep if she drank more mead, when she heard from the direction of the gate the sounds of a new arrival.

"My lady—" Dugech spoke from the door. "Are you still awake, Morgause?"

"Someone has come. I heard. Tell him to join the other drunkards in the hall—" she answered, lying back on her pillows again.

"But lady, it is your mother who is here!"

Morgause sat up, calculating swiftly the time it would have taken for a messenger to reach the Lake, and for Igierne to make the journey to Dun Eidyn. Did her mother have a spy here, as she herself did on the Isle of Maidens, or was it Ia, receiving the word from her brother, who had willingly or unwillingly let the high priestess know?

She swung her feet over the edge of the bed and reached for a shawl. Whatever the truth might be, she must suppress any reaction until she could find out why her mother was here.

Even the warmth of the firelight could not disguise the pallor of Igierne's skin, and Morgause was aware of an unexpected and surprisingly painful pang of fear. At times she had longed for the day when her mother would be gone and she should inherit her place on the Isle of Maidens. But not now, when she was battling to retain her hold on the Votadini. The idea that she might still long for her mother's love was a thought she could not allow.

"Bring us some chamomile tea, and show my mother's women where they will be sleeping," she told Dugech. Igierne had brought two priestesses whom Morgause did not know, an older woman and a dark-eyed girl with corn-colored hair, who were bringing in baskets and bundles.

"The burning was this morning. You missed it—" she said then. "Did you think I needed a shoulder to weep on? I am doing well. You did not have to make such a journey for my sake."

"Gracious as ever . . ." murmured Igierne, drinking from the cup of tea Dugech set before her. A little color began to return to her cheeks. "Perhaps I came to honor Leudonus."

"Since your son could not be bothered," said Morgause. "Or was Artor unable to come? I hear he has never quite recovered from his wounding two years ago, despite your attempts to heal him."

"He can ride—" Igierne answered, frowning. "Yet even if he could leave his army, the king would not have been here in time for the funeral. But I remember Leudonus in his youth, and even if you do not, I will mourn him. It was long since I had seen him, but he was one of the last men of Uthir's generation. The world is poorer for having lost him."

Morgause snorted and lifted a hand as men do to acknowledge a hit when they practice with swords. "Very well. But you cannot wonder that I am surprised to see you. We have not been close these past years."

"I will not quarrel with you regarding whose fault that is. I am too tired." Igierne set down her tea. "I had hoped that now you are a grandmother yourself, you might be able to put aside your resentment of me. . . ."

Morgause felt the color flood up into her face and then recede again. "What do you mean?"

"Gualchmai has a girl-child, did not you know? She is the daughter of some woman he met in the hills. She is twelve now. He sent her to me last year." At the words, the younger of her companions looked up, her eyes wide and dark as

those of a startled doe. "Come, Ninive, and greet your grandmother—"

Seen close to, Ninive was obviously a child, gazing around
her as if any sudden sound would send her bounding away.
A wild one, but I could tame her, thought Morgause as the girl
bent to kiss her hand. *Why did Gualchmai not give her to me?*

But at a deeper level, she knew. Her brother had stolen her
two elder sons already, and now her mother was claiming the
girl, the granddaughter that she could have trained as a
priestess in a tradition older than anything in Igierne's mysteries. Igierne had been foolish to bring her here, or foolishly
sure of her own power.

"You are very certain of her—" she said when Ninive had
been sent off for more tea. "It is not an easy life, there on the
island. What if the child wants a man in her bed and children
at her knee? She ought to have the chance to choose—"

"Why do you think I brought her here?" Igierne replied,
with that lift of the eyebrow that had always exasperated her
daughter, so eloquent in its assumption of authority.

For a moment, Morgause could only stare. "How generous!
Well, I will speak with Ninive after the assembly, and then
we will see if she takes after you, or me. . . . But I can see why
Gualchmai did not wish to bring a girl-child to Artor's court,"
she added reflectively.

"What do you mean?"

"My brother does not write to me, but others do," Morgause replied, "and there are many who say that the queen's
bed is not empty, though Artor does not lie there."

"It is not so—" said Igierne, but Morgause suppressed a
smile, seeing the uncertainty in her mother's eyes.

"Is it not? Well, I have no objection if Guendivar follows
northern ways. If the king is not potent, it is up to the queen
to empower the land."

"By taking lovers, as you have? Who fathered your sons,
Morgause?"

Morgause laughed, having goaded her mother to a direct
attack at last. "What man would dare to boast of having fathered a child on the queen, especially when it was not she
with whom he lay, but the Goddess, wearing her form, and

he himself possessed by the God? My children are more than royal, Mother, they are gifts of the gods!"

In the next moment she realized that this stroke had missed its mark. Igierne sat back and took another sip of tea.

"Ah—so that is how it came to pass. Beware, daughter, lest the gods call you to account for what you have made of their gifts to you."

Morgause frowned, aware of having revealed more than she meant to. But even if Igierne knew Medraut's parentage, what could she do? This child, at least, was her own, body and soul.

"You have had a long journey, Mother, and you must be weary," she said then. "And I must be fresh for tomorrow's assembly of the clans. Dugech will show you where you are to sleep." Morgause rose, summoning the woman who waited by the door. But despite her words, she herself tossed restlessly until the dawn.

Still, the gods had not abandoned her, for by the end of the council, the clans, while recognizing the claim of Dumnoval to lead the southern Votadini, and choosing Cunobelinus as warleader for the northern clans, had agreed that Morgause should continue to rule in Dun Eidyn as regent for Gualchmai. But Ninive chose to return to the Isle of Maidens with Igierne.

"They tell me that you are shaping well as a warrior." Morgause looked up at her fourth son as they stood on the guard path built into the rampart of Dun Eidyn. Goriat over-topped her by more than a head, and she was a big woman. Indeed, he towered over most men. She was not entirely certain who had fathered him, but as he grew it seemed likely that it was a man of Lochlann, who had come bringing furs and timber from the Northlands that lay eastward across the sea. She remembered the beauty of the trader's long-fingered hands.

"Men say that Gualchmai is the greatest warrior in Britannia. If I cannot surpass him, I have sworn to be the second." Goriat grinned.

"But are you the best fighter in Alba?" she asked then.

"I can take any man of the tribes—"

"South of the Bodotria," she corrected, "but you have not yet measured yourself against the men of the Pretani." Morgause gestured northward, where the lands of the Picts were blossoming in tender green beneath the sun.

Goriat shrugged. "If Artor fights them, I suppose I shall find out."

She looked up, startled by his tone. It was natural that he should think of following his brothers into his uncle's service, but she had not realized he considered it a certainty.

"Perhaps Artor will not have to fight them," she said carefully. "If one of his kindred is their warleader. . . . The Pretani have a princess of the highest lineage who is ripe for marriage. You know they seek outlanders to husband their royal women to avoid competition within the clans. They have sent a messenger, asking me for one of my sons. Marry the girl, and you will lead their armies and father kings."

"The Pretani!" Goriat exclaimed in revulsion.

"Alba!" Morgause replied. "If the Votadini and the Pretani make alliance, the north will be united at last!"

"And then may the gods pity Britannia!" He turned to face her, his long fingers curling into fists. "But it will not happen. If you think I will lend myself to this plot, Mother, you have gone mad. Play your games with Medraut, if you will, but I will stand on the other side of the board."

"You are an idiot without understanding," she hissed. "With one of my sons on the high seat of Britannia and my grandson on the sacred stone of the Pretani, we will rule this entire Hallowed Isle! You will go north, Goriat, or you will go nowhere! You think yourself a man and a warrior, but I am the Great Queen!"

Morgause turned and stalked away along the parapet, leaving him there. He was young and rebellious, but she held the purse-strings. His brothers had gone outfitted with arms and horses and servants as befitted their station, but her fourth son should have nothing until he agreed to do her will.

But the next morning, when she called for him, Goriat had disappeared.

For three days, Morgause raged. Then she began to think once more. For a time she considered sending Medraut to the

Picts instead, but he was not yet a warrior, although in other areas he was precocious enough to give her concern. Yet even if he had been of an age to marry, Medraut had a different destiny. At heart, Morgause, like Goriat, held Britannia to be the greater prize, and of all her sons, Medraut was the one with the greatest right to it.

At Midsummer, the tribes of the north celebrated the sun's triumph by clan and district, making the offerings and feasting and blessing their cattle and their fields. Each year, it had been the custom of the queen to keep the festival with a different clan, but the summer after the death of Leudonus, she gave out that this year she would observe the holiday in seclusion, and her youngest son with her, in honor of her lord.

A few days before the solstice they set out east along the shore of the firth, towards a headland with a house to which Morgause had often retired when she needed to recuperate from the demands made on a queen. Her folk were accustomed to this, and there was no surprise when she dismissed all attendants except Dugech and Leuku. But none knew that the following evening a boat was beached on the shore below, whose crew spoke with Pretani tongues, or that it pushed off once more before the sun was in the sky, bearing the queen of the Votadini, her maid Dugech, and her son.

"Why does Leuku not come with us?" asked Medraut as the land grew dim behind them.

"She will keep a fire going in the house so that any who pass will believe we are all still there."

For a few moments he was silent. "Does that mean we will be gone for some time?"

"For a space of several days. It is time you saw how folk who have not abandoned the most ancient ways of our people keep the festival."

Medraut's eyes brightened as he realized that she was at last going to share with him the secret of her mysterious journeys.

At thirteen, he had reached an uneasy balance between boy and man. He would never, she thought, have the height and sheer muscular power of his brothers. But the size of his hands and feet promised growth, and even now, at a boy's most awkward age, he had an agility that should develop into uncommon speed and grace. Gualchmai and Gwyhir and Goriat possessed physical splendor, while Aggarban, when last she saw him, had been cultivating a dark truculence that was impressive in its own way. Her youngest son would have an elegance that verged on beauty. Already, when he chose to do so, Medraut knew how to charm.

And sexual maturity was coming early as well. She had seen him bathing with the other boys, and though the fuzz on his cheeks was not yet worth shaving, his man's parts were full sized, surrounded by a bush of red hair. Medraut had an eye for women already, and only the most dire of threats to her maidservants had preserved his virginity thus far. Morgause would have preferred that he hold on to that power, but since chastity was probably unattainable, she meant to channel the magic of Medraut's sexual initiation through ritual.

"And in what way, Mother, are the rites of the Pretani different from Votadini ways?"

From his expression, Morgause could tell that there was something strange about her answering smile. "There is more blood in them," she said softly, "and more power."

The current had been with them, and the northern shore was already near. On the beach, horsemen were waiting. Morgause felt her pulse begin to beat more strongly. She took a deep breath, scenting woodsmoke and roasted flesh on the wind.

They came to Fodreu in the evening when the sun, still clinging to his season of triumph, turned the smoke from a multitude of cookfires to a golden haze. Coming over the rim of the hill they could see the gleam of water where the Tava curved abruptly eastward. Just above the bend was a ferry, with rafts to take them across the swift-running stream, and then they were following the road along the far bank towards the royal dun. Drest Gurthinmoch had emerged victorious from the turmoil following the death of Nectain Morbet and married the queen. He reigned now over the Pretani of both north and south from a stout dun near the sacred grove that held the coronation stone.

But that was another mystery. Today, their way led to the wide meadow where a women's enclosure had been prepared for the honored guests of the Pretani queen. Here, Morgause parted from Medraut, with certain words of warning to the warrior assigned to escort him. Then she passed through the gateway where Tulach was waiting to escort her to the queen.

The inner enclosure had been hung with woolen cloths embroidered with sacred symbols. Behind the queen's high seat the hanging stirred in the draught, so that the red mare pictured upon it seemed to move. Above it were images of the comb and mirror, symbols of the Goddess who ruled both in this world and the next. The queen herself wore red garments, also heavily embroidered, and was eating dried apples from a woven platter held by one of her maidens.

Uorepona—the Great Mare—was for her both a name and a title, always borne by the ruling queen. She was older than her husband, having been queen to Nectain Morbet before him, a little woman with grey hair, her body sagging with age.

Morgause made her obeisance, wondering nervously if Uorepona had loved her first husband, and if so, whether she might seek vengeance on the sister of the man who had killed him.

"The Great Mare of the Pretani bids you welcome," said Tulach in the British tongue.

"The Great Queen of the Votadini gives thanks, and offers her these gifts in token of her friendship," answered Dugech, motioning one of the slaves to bring forward the casket. Courtesy was all very well, but too much humility would be taken as weakness.

The atmosphere warmed perceptibly as Uorepona examined the ivory comb, the ornaments of golden filigree, and the vessels of Roman glass. A length of crimson silk was unfolded and immediately put to service as a mantle. The queen's woman offered Morgause apples from the platter, and she began to relax, understanding that as an accepted guest, she would be safe from now on.

"I have brought with me my son to be initiated into manhood—" she said later that evening as they sat around the women's fire. "He is the son of a king and comes of a line of warriors, and has never lain with a woman. I will give you the first offering of his seed if you have among your servants a clean maiden to receive it."

Uorepona spoke to her women in the Pictish dialect and laughed, by which Morgause concluded that though she did not speak British well, she understood it. When she had finished, one of the women replied.

"He is the bronze-haired lad that came with you, is it not so? My lady says that if she were younger she would take his seed herself, but as she is old, she will set her ornaments upon one of her servants to stand in her stead. The lady Tulach shall help you to choose . . ."

The Great Mare was served entirely by women. Even the slaves were of good blood, captives taken in war. Almost immediately, one of the girls caught Morgause's eye, a slim child scarcely older than Medraut, though her breasts were grown. But what had attracted the queen's attention was the bright red-gold of her hair and her amber eyes. She was very like Guendivar. . . .

"That one—" she gestured. "Where is she from?"

Tulach shrugged. "She is British, taken as a child in Nectain Morbet's war, but her lineage is not known."

Morgause nodded. "She will do very well."

The longest day continued endlessly beneath the northern sky. Earlier, the men had competed in contests of strength and skill, and the cattle had been driven through the smoke of the herb-laden fires. Now the sun was sinking, although it would be close to midnight before the last light was gone from the sky. The scent of cooking meat drifted through the encampment as the carcasses of sacrificed cattle roasted over many fires, but the smell of blood still hung in the air.

Tonight, the gods of the Pretani must be rejoicing, thought Morgause. Even the Votadini festivals were not so lavish, and as Christianity strengthened in the south, Artor's feasts had become bloodless travesties. A distant drum beat was taken up by others; her blood pulsed in time to the rhythm that throbbed in the air. Soon, the Goddess would receive another kind of offering.

Morgause had been given a place of honor with the women. On the other side of the circle she could see Medraut, sitting with the other boys. He had a gift for languages, and his agile tongue had clearly mastered the speech of the Pretani well enough to make them laugh. But from time to time his gaze would flicker towards her, questioning.

Trust me— She sent reassurance back with her smile. *This is for your good. You will see. . . .*

The slaves brought platters of meat still steaming from the spit, and skins of mead and heather beer. Some of the men were already becoming drunken, but what was given to the boys had been diluted. The ritual required that they be merry, but not incapable. Chieftains rose in place to boast of their achievements and praise the king. Young warriors marched into the center of the circle and danced with swords. And presently, after Drest's bard had completed a song in his honor, the drumbeat quickened, and the boys, with the awkward grace of colts just beginning their training, danced into the circle in a wavering line.

Morgause had spared no pains in her son's education. At this age, all boys were somewhat ungainly, but Medraut had not yet begun the growth spurt that would make his body for a time a stranger's, and in addition to her more private teaching, he had been rigorously schooled in running and leaping, in riding and in swordplay, and in the stylized movements of the warrior's dance.

It was a tradition the Votadini shared with their northern neighbors. Medraut's thin body took on grace as he recognized the quickening rhythm, spine straightening, shoulders braced, and the belted kilt that was all he wore swinging as his feet stamped in time. This was a tradition of unarmed combat. The beat shifted and the boys paired off, leaping and feinting with clenched fists or open hands, proud as young cocks of their energy and skill.

Skinny torsos shone with perspiration; differences in conditioning became apparent as some of the boys began to slow.

Medraut, who had learned a few movements not included in the formal sequence, leaned close to his partner as they switched positions, feet flickering, and in the next moment the other boy fell. Face flaming with shame, he pulled himself upright and shambled off to the sidelines to join those whose endurance had given out.

Again a shift in the drumbeat signaled a change, and the pairs became a line once more. Faster and faster the rhythm drove them, and the dancers circled and spun. Another boy fell, with no help from Medraut, and rolled away. The drumming crescendoed and fell silent. The boys stopped dancing, one or two of them sinking to their knees, chests heaving, as the power of the music let go. Medraut stood with his head up, perspiration running in glittering rivulets down his chest and sides. The hair that clung damply to his neck was the color of old blood, but he had the air of a young stallion that has won his maiden race and vindicated his breeding.

Now a shimmer of tinkling metal brought heads up, eyes widening. A line of young women was filing in, their garments sewn with bits of silver and bronze. Singing and clapping hands, they circled the boys, and then drew back, leaving the girl Morgause had chosen standing alone.

She moved along the line of boys, as if considering them. Her movements were stiff and her smile anxious, as if she were not quite certain she would be able to follow her instructions. Her bright hair, combed in a shining cape across her shoulders, stirred gently as she moved. The boys twitched and licked their lips as she passed them, and halted at last before Medraut, as she had been told to do.

Medraut's eyes widened, and his mother smiled. The ornaments the girl was wearing belonged to the Great Mare, but the gown was one he would recognize as her own, with her perfume still clinging to every fold. *When you take her in your arms you will see Guendivar's face, but it is my scent you will smell, and my magic that will bind you. . . .*

She had borne five strong sons in pain and suffering, and except for the last, she might as well have been a barren tree. One by one, Artor had seduced them away. Her granddaughter had been taken by Igierne. Medraut was all that remained to her, and she meant to use all her magic to make sure that the link between them stayed as strong as if the cord still connected him to her womb.

The maiden twirled before her chosen champion. From around the circle came a soft murmur of appreciation as she unpinned the brooch that held her garment at the shoulder and let it fall. The girls sang louder and she swayed, cupping her naked breasts in her two hands. They were small, but perfect, pale nipples uptilted beneath the necklet of amber and gold. Medraut's kilt stood out in a little tent before his thighs, and Morgause knew that the girl was arousing him.

The boy had been told what the reward would be if he did well in the dancing, just as the maiden had been told what to do. Did he understand how the act was accomplished? Surely no lad brought up in the dun could be ignorant—he had seen animals coupling, and humans as well, when the revelry became too drunken in the hall.

Seeing the admiration in Medraut's eyes, the girl smiled and held out her hand. He sent a quick glance of appeal towards his mother, who nodded. Then he allowed the maiden to lead him away to the bower that had been prepared for them. The other girls followed, singing, and the rest of the boys, relieved or resentful, went back to their place in the circle and began to tease the serving girls to give them more beer.

To the queens, they offered mead. Now that her son had met his challenge, Morgause could afford to relax. She accepted a beaker and drank deeply, tasting the fire beneath the sweetness and sighing as the familiar faint buzz began to detach her from the world.

The royal circle began to break up as they prepared to light the great bonfire that had been built in the center of the field where they had held the competitions earlier that day. The sun had set some time ago, and the half-light was fading, soft as memory, into a purple glow. In the east, the waning moon, late rising as an old woman, was just beginning to climb the sky.

Morgause got to her feet, taking a deep breath as the world spun dizzily around her. Her heartbeat pounded in her ears, or was it the Pictish drums she was hearing? Uorepona was retiring with her women, but Morgause felt desire rising within her. Since those few days during Leudonus' funeral, her courses had not come. Surely, if she worshipped the Goddess at the Midsummer fires, she would become fertile once more!

The drumming deepened. From the other end of the encampment a procession was coming, the light of torches danced and flickered across the grass. Morgause joined the throng that was forming a circle around the pyramid of logs. Tinder of all kinds had been stuffed within it, and the whole doused with oil. In times of danger, that frame of tinder would have held a man.

It will burn, she thought, taking her place in the circle, *and so will I. . . .*

Shouting, the torchbearers danced around the waiting pyre, rushing inward and then retreating once more. Again and again they surged, in and back and in again, while the first stars began to prick through the silken curtain of the sky. Each thrust was echoed by a cry from the crowd. The shouting got louder, the dance more frenzied, and Morgause swayed, feeling warmth kindle between her thighs. And then, as if the need of the gathered clans had driven them to climax, the dancers leaped forward and plunged their torches into the pyre.

The tinder caught, flame began to spark along the logs. Morgause felt a blast of warmth against her cheeks as fire billowed skyward. The drumming picked up and suddenly everyone was dancing. She laughed, whirling in place, and then began to move sunwise around the bonfire, hips swaying, arms outstretched.

One of the men caught her eye and began to dance with her, but she did not like his looks, and whirled away. Soon enough a bright-haired warrior found favor, mirroring her movements as they danced together, burning with the same flame. The dance brought them closer and closer, until her bobbing breasts brushed his chest. He seized her then, kissing her hungrily, and staggering like drunkards they wove among the other dancers until they reached the edge of the circle and collapsed together, bodies straining, on the grass.

Her warrior served her well, but when he had left her, Morgause still felt hunger. *Take me!* her heart cried as she began to dance once more, *fill me with your seed, and I will live forever!*

And soon another man came to her, and when she had exhausted him, a third. By this time, her clothing had gone, and she danced clad only in her own sweat and her necklaces of amber and jet. After that, she ceased counting. At one point she lay with two men together, and then, just as the early dawn was lightening the eastern sky, she enticed one of the drummers, for there were not many dancers left upright, though coupling figures still writhed upon the grass.

Morgause drew him down, pulling at his clothing with hasty caresses until he grunted and entered her. He was tired, and took his time at it, but a satiated exhaustion was finally overcoming her as well. She lay spread-eagled on the earth, quivering to his thrusts, until above his harsh breathing another sound caught her attention. She looked up, and gazing past the man's muscled shoulder saw Medraut, his hair glinting in the first light, disgust in his eyes.

"You are a man now—" Morgause said harshly. "This is what men do. Did you think you were so different?" Her partner groaned then and convulsed against her, and she laughed.

It was nearly noon when Morgause woke, her head throbbing from too much mead and her body aching from rutting in the grass. After she had bathed, she began to feel better and returned to the women's enclosure. Medraut was nowhere to be seen, but she recognized his maiden, working with the other slave girls to clear the detritus of the night's carousing away. She was wearing a bracelet that Morgause had last seen on her son's arm.

She ducked beneath the shade of the striped awning to pay her respects to the queen.

"Your son performed well last night," Uorepona said through her interpreter.

"He did. But now the girl may bear his child. Will you sell her to me?"

"If that is so, she would be all the more valuable," came the answer.

"I will be frank with you," said Morgause. "The children of princes must be begotten at the proper time and season. It is not my desire that there should be a child, nor that the vessel that received this holy sacrifice should be tainted by the use of one less worthy. But I cannot dispose of your property."

Uorepona bent to whisper into Tulach's ear.

"Ah—now I begin to understand you. But she is a pretty thing, and has been useful. If I had known your intention, I would have offered you a slave of less value."

"She was the best choice for my purpose," answered Morgause. "I will pay well."

Tulach nodded, and they began the delicate process of haggling.

For the two nights that remained of the festival, Medraut slept with the slave girl and hardly spoke to his mother at all. The girl herself had not been informed of the change of ownership, and when the time came for Medraut to depart, clung to him, weeping. The boy had already tried to persuade Morgause to bring the slave south with them and been refused. When at last they took the road towards the firth, there were tears in his eyes as well.

"Will we come back here? Will they be kind to her?" he asked as the grey waters of the Bodotria came into view.

"She will be well taken care of," answered Morgause, knowing that by now the slave collar would have been replaced by the mark of the strangler's cord. In time, she would tell Medraut that the girl was dead, and he would forget her.

"Why did you bring me here?" muttered the boy. "Every time something good happens to me, you take the joy away...."

"You are a prince. You must learn to master your desires."

"As you did at the festival?" he snapped back, then flushed and looked away.

Morgause took a deep breath, striving to control her temper. This was the child of her heart, and she must not drive him off. "I had a reason," she said finally. "What is important is not *what* you do so much as why."

"And you won't tell me. . . . Will you answer any of my questions? You have taught me things you never showed my brothers, and they are princes too!"

Morgause took a deep breath. Was now the moment she had been awaiting? Now, when he was beginning to understand what it meant to be a man?

"Your brothers are only princes of the Votadini. You are by birth the heir to all Britannia."

Medraut reined in sharply, all color draining from his face, staring at her.

"Your father and I lay together unknowing, god with goddess, in the sacred rite of the feast of Lugus. But the seed that was planted in my belly was that of Artor," Morgause said calmly. "In the old days, you would have been proclaimed before all the people, but Britannia is ruled now by Christians, who would count what we did a sin. Nonetheless, you are Artor's only child."

From pale, Medraut's face had flushed red. Slowly his complexion returned to normal, but his eyes were shining.

Oh my brother, thought Morgause, *you fathered this child, but I possess his soul. . . .*

A VESSEL OF LIGHT

A.D. 502

In THE SECOND YEAR OF THE NEW CENTURY, SICKNESS STALKED
the land. It came with vomiting and fever, and when it killed,
took by preference the young and strong. The first cases appeared in Londinium, where a few trading vessels still put in
at the wharves, and the illness spread along the roads to such
other centers of population as remained. Then it began to
strike in the countryside. If not so deadly as the great plague
that had devastated the empire some forty years before, it was
fearful enough to make people flee the towns that were beginning to rise from the ashes of the Saxon wars.

That year, the rains of winter persisted into the summer
months, blighting the grain. Those who were still healthy
shivered along with the sick and cursed whichever gods commanded their loyalty. And some, especially those who held
to the old ways, began to speak against the king.

Artor had never entirely recovered from the wound he got
in the Irish wars. He could walk and fight and ride, but not
for long. He had moved to Deva to direct the conclusion of
the campaigning, but he had delegated its execution to Agricola in Demetia, and Catwallaun Longhand in the north of
Guenet. And the British efforts had been rewarded with vic-

THE BOOK OF THE CAULDRON † 145

tory. Even the holy isle of Mona was now free. The only Irishmen remaining in Britannia were those who had given oath
to defend it for Artor—Brocagnus in Cicutio, and others farther inland. To Cunorix, who had once been his hostage, he
gave the defense of Viroconium, and the Irish mercenary Ebicatos was installed in Calleva.

But to the common folk of Britannia, coughing beneath
their leaky thatching and watching the rain batter down the
young grain, these great victories were distant and irrelevant.
Any warrior could kill enemies, but the power that kept
health in man and beast and brought good harvests came
from the king.

And the king, or so ran the rumor, was not a whole man.
For six years he had been married, and yet his young queen
bore no child. Merchants who braved the dangers of the road
to come to Camalot bore tales as well as cloth and knife
blades and spices. By his life or by his death, it was the duty
of the High King to heal the land.

Guendivar took a handful of coins from her pouch and
pushed them past the packets of herbs and spices to the peddler. There were more than the pepper and nutmeg, the hys-
sop and saffron and sandalwood warranted, but she would
not haggle. From the smile with which the old man took
them, he understood that she was paying for the information
as well.

If only, she thought as she gathered up her purchases in
the corner of her mantle and set off for the kitchen, she could
have acquired so easily some specific for the problems he had
described to her. She had gone to Cama's sacred spring to
pray, and learned only that she herself would be protected.
And last Beltain, she had gone, veiled, to the sacred fires
where the country folk still lit them in the hills, and allowed
a fair young man to draw her into the woods during the dancing, but she had not kindled from his lovemaking. This year,
it was likely to be too wet to even light the fire.

There was some lack in her, she thought sadly, as well as
in the king. For her to bear a child would have stilled wag-
ging tongues, no matter who the father might be. But she was

a barren field. Since Melguas had seduced her when she was his captive, Guendivar had lain with several men, but despite their caresses, she, whose body throbbed with pleasure at the warmth of the sun on her back or the feel of a cat's soft fur, had responded to none of them. Only with the folk of faerie did she feel fully alive, and her responsibilities often prevented her from seeking them. If Merlin had been with them, she would have begged him to teach her the mysteries she had once refused. But his absences had grown longer in recent years.

She regretted now that shame had kept her from touching the Cauldron. If she had had the courage, it might have healed her, and through her, the king. Artor had spoken sometimes of the Cauldron's power to renew the land. But in the condition he was now he could never spare the time it would take to travel back to the Lake.

She stopped short, still standing on the muddy path between the royal hall and the cookhouse, heedless of the fine rain that was scattering beads of crystal across her mantle and her hair. Artor could not go to the Cauldron, but could the Cauldron come here?

She did not believe that the king could be brought to appeal to his mother, even—or perhaps especially—if it concerned his own safety. But perhaps the Lady of the Lake would respond to a message from the High Queen.

A change in the wind brought her the scent of cooking, and Guendivar began to walk once more. If she wished to appeal to Igierne, she must find a messenger—not one of Artor's warriors, who would insist on getting confirmation from his commander, but someone with the strength and wit to make the journey swiftly, who would carry the message simply because it was the queen's desire.

Folk looked up, smiling, as she pulled open the door. Guendivar had never thought to be glad of her mother's training, but she did understand how to talk to the men and women who served her, and the cooks were always glad to see her, knowing she would make no demands without reason, and do her best to see that they had the resources they needed to do their job. As for the queen, she had noticed that males were more likely to be reasonable when they were well fed, and in this, Artor's champions were no different from any other men.

"A peddler has come, and I have bought out his store of spices—" She spilled the contents of her mantle out onto the scrubbed wooden table.

The chief of the cooks, a big, red-faced man called Lollius, set down his cleaver to look at them. The others clustered around him, chattering as the packets were identified, except for one lad, a strongly built fellow who was so tall he had to stoop to get through the door. He had looked up briefly when she came in, coloring to the roots of his fair hair, and then returned his attention to the bulbs of spear-leek that he was peeling. The sharp scent hung in the air.

That one—thought Guendivar. *He is in love with me.*

That, of course, was not unusual—half of Artor's men dreamed of her, or some fantasy that they gave her name. But this lad, who despite his northern burr spoke better than fit his station, seemed to look at *her*. She moved around the tables as the cook held forth upon the virtues and uses of the spices, examining a vegetable, or sniffing the contents of a bowl, until she stood beside him.

"Will the spear-leek go into the stew?" she asked softly.

"Lollius says it will fight sickness," he answered. "Surely it is strong enough!" He ventured a shy smile.

"You are very deft. What do they call you?"

"Manus—" He flushed again. "*Manus Formosus*," he added, "because of my hands."

"Indeed, they are very well-shaped and beautiful," Guendivar agreed. "But that is not the name your mother gave you, and you did not gain those shoulder muscles using a paring knife, but swinging a sword. Who are you, lad?"

At that, his clever fingers, which had continued to strip the papery rind from the bulbs, fell still.

"I have sworn not to say . . ." Manus answered finally, "until I have been in the king's service for a year and a day."

"That time is almost over," said the queen. She remembered his arrival now, though he had been much thinner then, as if he had been long on the road and lived hard. "When it is done, you will ask my lord for the boon he promised. But until then, your service belongs to me."

"Always..." he muttered, though he would not meet her eyes.

"I wish you to carry a message to the Lady of the Lake. But none must know where you go or why. Will you do that for me?" There was a short silence. One of the other servants began to hack vigorously at a peeled turnip, and she drew Manus after her to the end of the table, wondering if the young man had heard.

"My lady, I will go," Manus answered at last.

"I am too old to go racketing about the countryside this way..." said Igierne, twisting uncomfortably. The other priestesses she had brought with her from the Isle of Maidens moved around the room, unpacking clothing and hanging cloaks and mantles up to dry, for they had reached Camalot on the wings of an oncoming storm. But the chest at the foot of her bed they left strictly alone.

"Is the bed too hard?" Guendivar patted the pillows into shape as Igierne lay back again. The queen's bright hair was hidden by a veil, and there were smudges of fatigue beneath her eyes. What business did *she* have looking so tired, wondered Igierne? She had not travelled for two weeks in the rain.

"The bed is well enough, but every heartbeat jolts me as if I were still in that damned horse-litter," she snapped in reply. "I thought to find Artor on his deathbed at the very least, but aside from an indoor pallor and some weight around his middle that's due to lack of exercise, he seems well enough. So why did you summon me?"

"You know in what state he was when he left the Isle of Maidens." Guendivar frowned. "He may be no worse, but he is certainly no better. But that is not why I wrote to you. It is the land that is sick, and the people who are dying, and if you do not understand that, then why did you come?"

Igierne sighed, letting go of her anger. "Not entirely because of your message, so you need feel neither guilt nor pride. For the past moon I have had evil dreams...."

"Dreams of water rushing in a great wave, overwhelming the land?" asked Guendivar in a shaking voice.

Igierne raised herself on one elbow, remembering the potential she had once seen in this child—but no, Guendivar was twenty-one, a woman now. Was she at last beginning to grow into her power?

"Just so," she said softly. "I think it is one of the gifts of the queens to have such dreams. But the last of those dreams was different. With the water came a great light, and a voice that sang."

"I heard it too," whispered Guendivar, "though I could not understand the words. But the light came from the Cauldron."

Igierne nodded, her gaze moving involuntarily to the chest. In externals, it seemed no different than any of the others, though it was heavier because of the sheets of lead with which it was lined. Even so, she could feel the presence of the cauldron it held like a buzz along her nerves—perhaps it was that, and not the travel, that had made her so tired. Now she understood why it had always been kept within the shielding earth and stone of the shrine.

"What will you do with it?" the queen asked then.

"I do not know. The Goddess has not told me. We can only wait for her to show us Her will. . . ."

Throughout that night it rained steadily, and yet this was only the harbinger of a storm such as the West Country had rarely known, driven straight from the Hibernian Sea. In the levels below the Isle of Glass the sea-swell would be backing up the rivers and making islands of the high ground. Guendivar could imagine how the marsh-folk must be taking refuge on the Tor while the monks and the nuns chanted desperate prayers to their god.

In the sheltered lowlands, the waters were rising, but on the heights, one felt the full force of the wind. Artor's walls were small protection. The storm swept over the ramparts of Camalot to pluck at the thatching of the buildings within. Of them all, only the great round henge hall that Merlin had designed was entirely undamaged, though drafts swept through its wicker partitions and it flexed and shuddered with each onslaught of the storm. Father Kebi, the Christian priest who had spoken darkly of sorcery when the hall was being built, came meekly enough to take refuge with the others, though he crossed himself when he passed through the door. It was not council season, and many of Artor's chieftains were home on their own lands. With his Companions and his servants and the priestesses from the Isle of Maidens inside, there was just room for them all.

All that afternoon, Guendivar worked with her maidservants to bring food and drink and bedding, and then there was nothing she could do but take her place beside Artor, and force herself to keep smiling as she watched the torch flames flicker in the draught, and wait for the dawn.

Igierne shivered, wondering if the touch she had felt on her cheek had really been a drop of water. With her mind, she knew the hall would not fail them—she could sense Merlin's magic, binding post to pillar and thatching to beam— but her gut was not so certain. Ceincair helped her to settle her mantle more securely around her shoulders, and she thanked her, searching the crowd for her other priestesses as she turned.

"Where is Ninive?"

"She went to the side door, to relieve herself, she said, though I think she really wanted to see the storm," said Ceincair.

Igierne shook her head with a sigh. Bringing the child here had been a risk—in three years Ninive had learned a great deal, but she was still a woodscolt at heart, and if at times she found the serene society of the Isle of Maidens too confining, she must be suffering in this crowded hall. She was young and would take no harm from a wetting, but her absence was not the true cause of the priestess' unease.

It was the Cauldron.

Igierne had believed that the Goddess wanted her to bring it south, but what if her own concern for Artor had deceived her? In Eriu they had a tale of a woman who insulted a sacred spring and caused a flood that drowned the land. Was this a natural storm, or by taking the Cauldron from its spell-shielded sanctuary had she so unbalanced the elements that they would destroy Britannia? If it were required, she would take up the Cauldron with her own two hands and carry it to the sea, but she did not know what she ought to do. If the stakes had not been so high, Igierne would have accepted her panic as a necessary lesson in humility, but as it was, all she could do was close her eyes and pray.

"Lord have mercy upon us, Christ have mercy upon us," muttered the little priest as the storm raged. Betiver, who had hardly said a prayer since his childhood, found himself murmuring an echo, and so did many another of those who had been raised in Roman ways. A flare of lightning outlined the great door, and in another moment thunder clapped and rattled above them. Behind him, he heard men calling on Jupiter and Taranis and even Thunor of the Saxons.

He stiffened, veins singing with the same mingled fear and fury he felt before battle, and instinctively his gaze sought the royal high seat and his king. Artor, every nerve strained at attention as he waited for the next bolt to fall, nonetheless looked far better than the lethargic figure of yesterday. This was the valiant commander Betiver remembered from a hundred campaigns. Guendivar said something, and Artor leaned close to answer her, smiling and reaching out to grasp her hand.

It was almost the first time Betiver could remember seeing the king touch her, but before he could wonder, the lightning and thunder crashed around them once again.

Guendivar felt the warm strength of Artor's grip and squeezed back convulsively as the thunder shook the hall.

Lady, help us! For the sake of the king, for all this land! I will do whatever you ask, but I pray you, shelter us now!

She had never been afraid of thunderstorms, but this one had an unexpected and elemental power. Each flare of lightning showed clearly the unimportance of her own fears and frustrations. There was a life in the storm that had nothing to do with the problems of the queen of Britannia. Oddly enough, that relieved her. She sat, a still point in the midst of fury, rooted to the earth by the steady grip of her husband's hand, and waited for the next convulsion of the skies.

This time, the lightning's flare and the thunder were almost simultaneous. The hall trembled, the great doors sprang wide. Wind howled and every torch was extinguished, but in the same moment a blue iridescence burst through the opening and whirled about, edging post and beam and benches alike with livid light.

"It is Pentecost!" cried Father Kebi, "and the Holy Spirit has come to us in wind and fire!"

But the lightning passed, and the raging of the heavens was replaced by a sudden singing silence. They were in the eye of the storm. They sat, staring, while the blood beat in their ears, and the lightning focused to a single sphere of radiance that floated slowly around the interior of the hall. So bright it was that no man could say who bore it, or if indeed it moved by any human agency at all.

Guendivar stared at that brightness and knew that she was weeping, though she made no sound. From one person to another it passed, pausing for a few moments and then moving on, awarding as much time to a chieftain as to a serving lad, and to the woman who fed the pigs as to the priestesses who had come with Igierne. She saw it surrounding Julia, who crossed herself and then reached out, her cheeks shining with tears.

What are you? Who are you? the queen's heart cried as the light drew closer. Now it seemed to her that forms moved within that radiance; a procession of bright beings was passing through the hall. *What do you want from me?*

And then it was before her, swallowing up all other sensation except the pressure of her husband's hand.

An answer came. *"I am as full of wonders as Faerie, and as common as day. I am what you most desire. Now I stand before you, but only when I stand behind you will you understand Me truly, and be fulfilled."*

And then it seemed to her that the light shimmered, and she glimpsed within it a woman's form. The radiance surrounded her, and she tasted sweetness beyond the capacity of mortal food, though she never afterward was able to say if it had been truly taste instead of sight or sound.

Betiver heard singing, as he had heard it in the great church of Saint Martin as a child. With it came the sweetness of frankincense, filling the hall in great smoking clouds of light. The brightness drew closer, surrounded by a shifting glimmer like the movement of mighty wings. For a moment then he glimpsed a Chalice, through whose pure curve a rose-red radiance glowed.

"*I am thy true Lord and thy Commander. Follow Me!*"came a soundless Voice, and Betiver's spirit responded in an ecstasy of self-offering—

"I am Thy man until my life's end. How shall I serve Thee?"

"*Serve Britannia . . . serve the King. . . .*" came the answer, and he bowed his head in homage.

"Always . . ." he murmured, "always, wherever the road may lead. . . ."

To Igierne, alone among all that company, the visitation had a tangible form. She saw the glowing silver and knew it for the Cauldron, but as it approached, the image of the Goddess grew out of the low relief of its central panel to a full figure that expanded until it filled the hall.

"Brigantia, Exalted One, power upwelling—" she whispered, "watch over Your children."

"*When have I failed to do so? It is you who turn away from Me . . .*"

"Did I do wrong to bring the Cauldron to the king?"

"*You did well, though a time will come soon when you will question that choosing. But for now, be comforted, for in the flesh your son has his healing, though he will not be whole in spirit until he sees Me in another guise.*"

The radiance intensified, growing until she could no longer bear its brilliance, carrying her to a realm where the spirit and the senses were one, and she knew no more.

*   *   *

To each soul in that circle the Cauldron came, after the fashion in which he or she could see it most clearly, and each one received the nourishment, in body and in spirit, that was most desired.

And presently folk began to blink and stir, gazing around them as if the painted pillars and the woven hangings, their own hands and each other's faces were equally strange and wonderful. It was no supernal radiance that showed them these things—that Light had disappeared. But the great door to the hall still stood open, and beyond it glowed a clear, rose-tinted sky, and the first golden rays of the rising sun.

Betiver looked exalted, as a warrior who has seen his victory. It was an expression that illuminated the faces of many of Artor's Companions, though they gazed around them now in confusion and loss.

"I had it—" whispered someone, "I almost understood—where has it gone?"

Igierne lay still, with her priestesses around her, but her breast rose and fell, and Guendivar knew that in time she would wake, restored. Father Kebi was murmuring prayers, on his face an unaccustomed peace. The cooks and the kitchen slaves gazed about them in amazement. But Manus' eyes shone like two stars.

Guendivar turned to her husband, understanding that she had seen the thing that was behind the faerie-folk who had once so enchanted her, and the source of their magic, though the images were fading so swiftly that she could no longer say just what it had been.

"What did you see, Artor?" she whispered. "What did you see?"

But he only shook his head, his eyes still wide, half-blinded by looking on too much light. She reached out, and he drew her to him and held her close against his heart, and for that moment, both of them were free.

Morgause gazed at the glory of the new day and cursed the gods. A night of elemental fury, followed by a dawning that might have belonged to the morning of the world, could only mean that Igierne had unveiled the Cauldron. The mysteries Morgause had studied during these past years had taught her how to sense the cycles of the land as once she had charted her own moontides, and she knew that this had been no natural storm. Such lore as she had been able to glean in the years she spent on the Isle of Maidens suggested that the precautions with which the Cauldron had always been surrounded were not only intended to control access to it— they were needed to control its power.

On the night just past they had surely seen the result of letting that power flow free. The ground was littered with leaves, and the woodlands were striped with pale slashes where entire branches had been torn from the trees. As the horses picked their way along the muddy trackway towards Camalot, she saw that the homes of men had fared even worse. Huts stood like half-plucked chickens, the bracing of their roofs bared where the thatching had been torn away. At that, the Celtic roundhouses, whose frames flexed with the storm, had fared better than the square-built Roman dwellings, which tended to crumble when the wind ripped off their terra-cotta tiles.

For anyone caught in the open, as she and her escort had been, the hours of darkness had been a nightmare. The cloak Morgause wore still steamed with moisture. Only the yew wood in which they had found shelter had saved them from an even worse battering by the storm.

And then, in the most secret hours before the dawning, the wind had dropped. For a few moments Morgause had wondered if the fury of the storm had transcended her powers of hearing. Then the air grew warmer, and she knew that the stillness betokened a Presence and no mere lack of sound.

Until then, she had hoped her suspicions might be mistaken. Her spy in Artor's kitchens knew only that Guendivar had summoned the Lady of the Lake. But in her dreams Morgause had seen the Cauldron rising like a great moon above the land. And so she had come south—but not swiftly enough to prevent her mother from bringing the Cauldron—the Hallow that was Morgause's birthright—to Artor.

This smiling morning only confirmed her in her conclusion. She felt orphaned; she felt furious. She had learned much from the witches of the Pretani, and yet she was a foreigner among them, always conscious that they kept secrets she could never learn. With the Cauldron, she could face them as an equal. During the past few years her desire for it had grown from an irritation to an obsession. It had to be hers!

There was no point in following her mother to Camalot and confronting her—the damage was done. Still, Igierne must leave eventually. Better, Morgause thought now, to keep her presence in the area a secret. Just ahead, the road had been washed out by the storm. Any party attempting to return to the Lake from the south must detour through the woodland. The damaged forest could hardly have been better arranged for setting an ambush. Limbs of alder and oak littered the ground, while sallow and willow had bowed to the blast. The marsh grasses were half submerged and the higher ground muddy. At her feet a marigold nodded in the light breeze. Morgause wondered how it had escaped the fury of the storm.

"We will stop here," she told her men. "Uinist, set a watch and send scouts around the woods to watch the southern road. Doli, it will be your task to position the men where they can attack successfully. And when we have finished, we will flee westward. If there is suspicion, they will be searching the main road that leads north from Lindinis. No one will expect us to skirt the higher ground and push towards the sea."

They had three days to wait before her men reported a large party coming up the road from the direction of Camalot. The horselitter, Morgause knew, must be carrying her mother. But even without the scouts she would have known who, and what, was coming—she could *feel* the presence of the Cauldron, as if its recent exercise had increased its power. She could feel it, and she wanted it, as a thirsty man desires the well.

Morgause ordered her men to do no harm to the Lady of the Lake. Far better, she thought vengefully, to let her mother live with the knowledge of what she had lost, as she herself had had to live without her birthright. The others they might kill, so long as they carried off all of the baggage and gear.

And so she waited while her men disappeared into the woodland, and just past the hour of noon, she heard women screaming and northern warcries, and smiled.

"Mother, it was not your fault!" Artor grasped Igierne's hands, chafing them. "Were it not for my weakness, the Cauldron would never have left the Isle of Maidens."

"It was my message that brought you—" echoed Guendivar.

"—but my decision to respond . . ." Igierne forced out the words.

She was still shivering, as she had ever since the attack. The men of her escort had been killed, but Ninive had caught one of the horses and galloped back to Camalot for help. That had been at midmorning, and now it was nearly eventide. The Cauldron was gone, and since Uthir's death, she had known no greater disaster. Ceincair wrapped blankets around her and spoke of shock, but Igierne knew it was fear.

"But who *were* they?" asked Aggarban.

"Men, with spears and bucklers and shirts of hardened leather," answered Nest. "The only words I heard were in British as we speak it in the north, but not the Pictish tongue. They could have been reivers, or masterless men."

"I thought all such had been hunted down by the king's soldiers," said Guendivar.

Artor's eyes flickered dangerously. "So did I . . ."

"It does not matter who they are—we must be after them!" exclaimed Gualchmai. "If that was indeed the Cauldron that by the power of the gods came shining through the hall, I would give my heart's blood to see it again!"

"And I!" said Vortipor. Other voices echoed his vow.

When the priestesses returned to the House of Women after that night of storm and glory, they had found the Cauldron safe in its chest, and no one could be brought to admit having touched or moved it. But what else could it have been? Now it was gone, and Igierne shuddered to think of the disaster it might bring in hostile hands.

She coughed and tugged at Ceincair's sleeve. "Did you note, among the riders, any women?"

"I did not," answered the priestess. "Do you think that Morgause—" She fell silent, seeing Gualchmai's stricken gaze.

"Do you think it is not as hard for me to say it, grandson, as for you to hear?" asked Igierne. "But your mother has always desired the Cauldron. In your searching do not forget the northern roads." *And if she has taken it, the fault is mine—* her thought continued. *Morgause begged me to teach her its mysteries, and I refused.*

"We will search *all* the roads, Mother," said Artor. She heard him giving orders as she sank back into the shelter of her blankets.

"And we will take care of you here," added Guendivar, "where you can hear the reports as the searchers come in."

Igierne shook her head. "The quest must take place in the mortal realm, and it is the High Queen, the Tigernissa, who is for your warriors the image of the Goddess in the world. I will go back to the Lake . . . I should never have left it, for I am Branuen, the Hidden Queen, and the quest of the spirit must be directed from there. Perhaps the Cauldron will hear our prayers and make its own way home."

THE QUEST

A·D· 502

Of those who had ridden out from Camalot in search of the Cauldron, the first to return was Betiver. When he came in, Guendivar was in the herb hut, stripping the tender leaves from mints she had gathered in the woods. The sharp, sweet fragrance filled the air.

"Where is the king?" he asked when he had saluted her.

"He rode over to Lindinis. He should be back for the evening meal."

"The king is riding?" he asked, astonishment sharpening his tone.

"He is much better," Guendivar said softly, "and the weather has been fine as well. If anyone doubts that what we saw was holy, surely its works speak for it."

"*I* do not doubt it, though I believe that vision is all that I shall ever see—" He sank down upon a bench, the glow which his eyes always held when he looked at her intensifying. "Perhaps that is why I do not feel compelled to continue trying to see it again."

"What do you mean?" she asked, watching him closely.

"When the Light came to me, what I saw within it was the Chalice of our Lord, and I was fed, and made whole. We have no assurance that the wonder that moved through the hall was the Cauldron. Igierne's priestesses say they did not take it from its chest, so how could it account for such a miracle?"

Guendivar frowned thoughtfully. Igierne had told her that she saw the figure of a goddess emerge from the Cauldron, while Julia's vision, like that of Betiver, had been of the chalice of the Christian mass. She herself had seen only luminous forms in a haze of light, and no vessel at all.

"The others who have gone said that the vision left them with an aching desire to see it again . . ." she said then.

"That is so, but when I had gone away, I found that all I truly longed for was here."

For a moment Betiver's gaze held hers, and she flinched, seeing his unvoiced love for her naked in his eyes. She had become accustomed to recognizing lust or longing when men looked at her. One or two had threatened to seek death in battle when she would not return their passion. Only Betiver seemed able to love her without being unfaithful either to his concubine in Londinium or to his king. She had not realized what a comfort that steady, undemanding devotion was until she noted her own happiness at seeing him back again.

His tone flattened as he went on, "But the theft of the Cauldron must not go unpunished, whatever its nature may be. I have sent word to all our garrisons, and set a watch upon the ports, and having done so, see no purpose in continuing to wander the countryside when I could better serve Britannia by helping Artor."

"The king will be grateful," Guendivar said carefully, "and so will I. It has been very quiet here, and lonely, with all of you gone."

The power of the Cauldron grew with the waxing of the moon. As Morgause and her men worked their way cross-country along the edges of the sodden lowlands, travelling by night and lying up during the day, she found herself constantly aware of its presence, as even with eyes closed, one can sense the direction of a fire. But this was a white flame, cool as water, seductive as the hidden current in a stream. She could feel her moods change as they had done before her moon cycles came to an end. At some times the smallest frustration could drive her to fury or tears, and at others, and these were ever more frequent as the moon grew from a silver sickle towards its first quarter, she was uplififted on a tide of joy.

Slowly, for the paths were rough and they often had to backtrack and find a new path, they travelled westward. Presently the folded hills with their meadows and patches of woodland gave way to a high heathland where a constant wind carried the sharp breath of the sea. In the days of the empire, these hills had been well populated, for Rome needed the lead from Britannia's mines. But most of the shafts had been worked out or abandoned when the trade routes were interrupted, and grass grew on the piled earth and rock where they had been.

Morgause and her party moved more openly now, taking the old road to the mouth of the Uxela where the lead ships used to come in. Only once did they pass a huddle of huts beside a working mine shaft, and no one greeted them. At the rivermouth they saw the remains of the port, which now was home only to a few fishermen whose boats were drawn up on shore. Saltmarsh and mudflat stretched along the coast to either side of the narrow channel; at low tide the atmosphere was redolent with their rank perfume. But when it changed, the waters surged up the estuary of the Sabrina, bringing with them fresh sea air and seabirds crying on the wind.

And there, as if the gods themselves had conspired to help her, a boat was waiting.

"Go to the captain and ask where he comes from and what he carries," she told Uinist. "If he is loading lead to take to Gallia say no more, but if he is sailing northward, ask if he will accept a few passengers."

Morgause had meant to follow the estuary and strike across country from there, but as her awareness of the Cauldron grew, it had come to her that perhaps Igierne would be able to trace the movement of power. If the Cauldron were at sea, surely its identity would be masked by that of the element to which it belonged.

And so it was that Morgause took ship with three of her men while the others turned back with the horses, travelling in groups of two and three to divert any pursuers who might have traced them.

Aggarban returned to Camalot on a stretcher. Hearing the commotion, Guendivar came running from the hall. For a moment she thought they had brought her a corpse to bury, then she saw his chest rise and fall.

"We heard there were strange riders in the hills to the west," said Edrit, the half-Saxon lad whom Aggarban had taken into his service. "We caught up with them just as night was falling, and when they would not stop, we fought. In the confusion, my lord and I were separated. It took me too long to kill my man, and by the time I found my way back it was full dark. There was a dead man in the clearing, but I had to wait until morning to track my master. He was lying in his blood with the body of his opponent beside him. I bound up his wounds as best I could, and then I had to find a farm with a cart to bear him. I am sorry, my lady—" He gazed at her with sorrowful eyes. "I did the best I could. . . ."

"I am sure you did," she said reassuringly, one eye on the old woman, of all their folk the most skilled in treating injuries, who was examining Aggarban.

"He was unconscious when I found him," Edrit babbled on, "and by the time I came back with the cart, he was burning with fever. But now that we are here he will better. You will heal him, lady, I know!"

"If God wills it—" she answered cautiously, but he was looking at her as if she were the Goddess, or perhaps only the Tigernissa. Only now was Guendivar beginning to understand that for some, that was almost the same thing.

The healer had finished her examination

"Will he recover?" she asked.

"I believe so, with time and careful nursing," the woman answered her. "He can make back the blood he has lost, and his wounds are not too severe. But I don't like that fever."

No more did Guendivar, but she had promised Edrit that she would try to save his master. For three nights she took turns with the other women to sit by the wounded man, sponging his brow and listening to his mutterings, until the crisis came.

It was past midnight, and the queen herself was half asleep in her chair, when a groan woke her.

"Hold!" Aggarban spoke quite clearly but his eyes were closed. "Don't trouble to deny it—I know ye for a northern man. Is my mother tangled in this business?" There was a silence, as if someone invisible were answering, and then, once more, that terrible groan. When he spoke again, his voice was softer, edged by pain.

"Ah, my mother, you were in the Light that came through the hall—and then you abandoned us. Do you not care for your sons? But you never did, save for that red-haired brat. Festival-bastard, king's-get—oh, I have heard the tales. Can you name *any* of our fathers?" The accusations faded into anguished mutterings.

"Aggarban—" The queen wrung water from the cloth and laid it on his brow. "It's all right now, it's over . . . you must sleep and get well."

His eyes opened suddenly, and it seemed that he knew her. "Queen Guendivar . . . you shine like the moon . . . and are you faithless too?"

She recoiled as if he had struck her, but his eyes had closed. He stopped speaking, and after a few moments she took a deep breath and laying her hand on his brow, found it cool. Guendivar rose then and called the healer to examine him; and after, she went to her own bed, and wept until sleep came.

It was sunset, and the moon, now in its first quarter, hovered halfway up the sky. To Morgause, sitting on a coil of rope beside the stern rail, it looked like a cauldron into which all the light was trickling as the sky dimmed from rose to mauve and then a soft violet blue. When her gaze returned to the sea, she saw the undulating landscape before her, opalescent with color, its billows refracting blue and purple as they caught the light and subsiding into dusk grey when they fell.

The ship flexed and dipped, angling across the waves towards her evening anchorage. She was called the *Siren*, and in a week of travel Morgause had come to know her routine. Unless the weather was exceptionally fine and the wind steady, they put in each night at some sheltered cove, trading for fresh food and water and exchanging news. In these remote places there had been no rumor of the search for the Cauldron, but even here folk had felt the storm and rejoiced in the peace that came after. Those who had not died of the great sickness were on the mend, and hope had returned to the land.

At first, such interrupted progress had frustrated Morgause to the edge of rage. If the first few villages had been able to sell them horses, she would have left the ship and gone overland—to struggle with the hazards of the mountains would have matched her mood. But as day succeeded day, ever changing and always the same, she found her anger dissolving away. Even the presence of the Cauldron did not disturb her, for at sea, she was in its element and there was no separation between them.

Moving across the surface of the waters, suspended between earth and heaven, she found herself suspended also between the time before she took the Cauldron and whatever the future might hold. Her desire for the Cauldron was unchanging, but she wondered now why she had fought so hard to rule the north? Beside its reality, even her ambitions for Medraut paled. She was beginning to understand that whatever happened now, the woman who returned to the north would not be the same as the one who had ridden away a moon ago.

Vortipor rode in to Camalot with ravens wheeling around him. When those who came out to welcome him realized that the round objects dangling from his saddlebow were severed heads, they understood why.

The man who had taken them was brown and healthy and grinning triumphantly. The heads were rather less so, and even Vortipor did not protest too much when Artor tactfully suggested that Father Kebi might be willing to give them Christian burial.

"Though I doubt very much that they deserve it. I was outnumbered, and could not afford them time to confess their sins." He did not sound sorry.

"I trust that they deserved the death you gave them—" Artor observed, but the steel in his tone did little to dim the young man's smile.

"Oh, yes. The cave where they held me was littered with the remains of *their* victims. We'll have to send a party to give them a grave as least as good as that of their murderers."

"They were robbers, then," said Guendivar.

"Most certainly, but they bit off more than they could chew when they captured me! I am sorry, my lady, that I have no news of the Cauldron, but when the Light passed through the hall, what I saw was a Warrior Angel, and I can only serve the truth I see...."

"None of us can say more than that," answered the king, and led him into the hall.

Even on dry land the ground seemed to be heaving. Morgause stumbled and halted, laughing. The *Siren* had put them ashore on the north bank of the Belisama, for her master would sail no farther. A half-day's journey would set them on the Bremetennacum road. It was far enough—no one would think to look for the fugitives here. Indeed, the fear of pursuit had ceased to trouble her, as had any ambivalence regarding her theft of the Cauldron.

It was *hers*, as the gods had always intended, and the time to claim her inheritance had arrived. When Doli began to ask her about the next stage of their journey, she waved him away.

"We can take thought for that tomorrow. Tonight is the full of the moon. Carry the chest up the beach—there, beyond the trees—and let no one disturb me." He was a Pict, and she knew he would not question his queen.

The sun was already sinking into the western sea, and as they reached the spot Morgause had chosen, a rim of silver edged the distant hill.

Swiftly she stripped off her clothes and stood, arms lifted in adoration, as the silver wheel of the moon rolled up the eastern sky. It had been long since she had saluted the moon with the priestesses, but she still remembered the beginning of their hymn.

"Lady of the Silver Wheel, Lady of the Three-fold Way . . . " For a moment she hummed, trying to recall how the next lines ran, then words came to her—*"Thy deepest mysteries reveal, hear me, Goddess, as I pray!"* She repeated the phrase, sinking deeper into the chant, finding new verses to continue the song.

Words of power she sang, to confirm her mastery, but gradually it seemed to her that she was hearing other voices and singing the old words after all, and she did not know if they came from memory, or whether the familiar melody had somehow linked her in spirit to the priestesses who even now would be drawing down the moon on the Holy Isle.

"Holiness is your abode . . . Help and healing there abound. . . ." But Morgause had not wanted healing, only power.

"Ever-changing, you abide . . . Grant us motion, give us rest. . . ." As she sang the words, her strength left her and she sank down onto her scattered clothing, her breath coming in stifled sobs. It took a long time before she could find a stillness to match that of the night around her.

And all that while, the moon had continued to rise. Morgause sat watching it, and draped her mantle over her naked shoulders against the night chill. She realized gradually that the quiet was a breathing stillness, compounded of the chirring of frogs, the gentle lap of the waves against the sand, and the whisper of wind in the grass. And now, as she watched, she saw the first spark of light on the water, and the moon, lifting ever higher, began to lay down a path of light across the sea.

Ripple by ripple the moonpath lengthened. Moving with dreamlike slowness, Morgause rose, undid the hasps that had secured the chest, and raised the lid. White silk swathed the Cauldron. Gently she folded it back, and drew in her breath at the glimmer of silver inside. It was as bright as if newly polished. The priestesses on the Isle of Maidens used to whisper that it never grew tarnished or needed to be cleaned.

For a moment longer awe kept her from moving, then she lifted the Cauldron and carried it to the water's edge. The tide was fully in, and she had not far to go. The moon was high, serene in a sky of indigo, so bright that the sea showed deep blue as well, but moving across the river came a dancing glitter of light. Still holding the Cauldron, Morgause waded into the water, and when it lapped the tops of her thighs, she lowered the vessel and let it fill.

Here, where the outflow of the river met the tide, the water was both sweet and salt. *It is all the waters of the world*, thought Morgause, bearing the Cauldron back to the shore.

She set it down at the water's edge and knelt behind it. A last wave ran up the sand and splashed her, and then the tide began to turn, but the moonpath continued to lengthen, glistening on the wet sand, until the light struck first the rim of the Cauldron and then the water within, and began to glow.

It was the power she had glimpsed in her mother's ritual, increased a thousandfold. It was all she had ever hoped for, or desired. Heart pounding, Morgause gripped the rim of the Cauldron and looked in.

In the first moment, she saw only the moon reflected in the surface of the water. In the next, light flared around her. She did not know if the water had fountained or she were falling in. Glowing shapes moved around her; she blinked, and recognized the goddesses whose outer images had been embossed upon the Cauldron's skin. The Lady of the Silver Wheel and the Lady of Ravens, the Flower Bride and the Great Mother, the Lady of Healing and the Death Crone, all of them passed before her—but now she perceived them without the veils of form that human minds had imposed to shield eyes unready to gaze on glory.

Morgause floated in the center of their circle, trembling as one by one they turned to look at her. She tried to hide her face, but she had no hands, and no feet with which to run even if there had been anywhere to go. A naked soul, she cowered beneath that pitiless contemplation that beheld and judged every angry thought and selfish deed and bitter word.

In that brilliance all her justifications and excuses dissolved and disappeared.

And with them, the separate images dislimned and flowed together until there was only one Goddess, who wore her mother's face, and gazed at her with all the love that Morgause had ever longed for in Her eyes, and then that image also gave way to a radiance beyond all forms and gender, and she knew no more.

Half a hundred of Artor's Companions had ridden out to search for the Cauldron. As the infant moon grew to maturity and then began to dwindle, more and more of them returned. Some, like Aggarban, came back wounded. Sullen and taciturn once his fever left him, Aggarban was recovering well, but there were others who reached Camalot only to die, or who never returned at all, and Guendivar could not help but wonder whether Morgause had managed to curse the Cauldron.

And yet there were others who came back with a new light in their eyes, having found, if not the Cauldron, the thing that gave it meaning. It had taken her some days to realize that Manus, who had accompanied Igierne back down from the north, had gone out to search with the other men. He had not returned either, but she could not explain why she was worried about a kitchen lad.

The days passed, and Cai came in. He seemed more peaceful than he had been, though he refused to say much of his journey.

"I never even found a trace of the theives," he told them. "But I do feel better—perhaps I just needed to get away...."

Peretur had a strange tale of a girl he met by a sacred spring that made Guendivar wonder if he too had encountered the folk of faerie. Gwyhir returned triumphant, having surpassed Vortipor's tally of slain outlaws. Young Amminius did not come back, but sent word that he was leaving the world to join a hermit he had found in the forest.

By the dark of the moon, of the most notable warriors all had been accounted for save Gualchmai. At first, Artor refused to worry. His nephew was widely recognized as the best fighter in an army that was the best in Britannia. Surely he could deal with any foe who might challenge him. But as time went on with no word, men began to remember that even the greatest fighter could be taken down from ambush or overwhelmed by numbers. And yet, even outnumbered, Gualchmai must have given an account of himself that would make the heavens ring.

And then, as the first sliver of new moon glimmered in the afternoon sky, the gate guard sent word that a single rider was coming up the road, a big man with a shock of wheat-colored hair. That hair, and the red-and-white shield, were famous all over Britannia. By the time Gualchmai rode through the gate, the entire population of Camalot was turned out to meet him.

"What is it?" he asked, looking around him. "Is there a festival?"

Whatever he had been doing, it was not fighting, for there was not a mark upon him. In fact he looked younger. The tunic he was wearing was new, made from green linen with embroidery around the neck and hems.

"To look at you, there must be!" exclaimed Gwyhir. "Where have you been, man? We've been worried about you!"

"Oh . . ." A becoming flush reddened Gualchmai's skin. "I didn't realize." There was another pause. "I got married . . ." he said then.

He could hardly have caused a greater uproar, thought Guendivar, if he had announced a new invasion of Saxons. In time of war, Gualchmai was a great fighter. In peace he had gained an equal reputation as a lover of women. One could believe almost any feat in the bedchamber or the battlefield. But not marriage.

He told them about it later, when they were all gathered in the hall. He had taken the northern road, and after a day found the tracks of a large party of men. Gualchmai followed them onto a path that led through a patch of woodland, catching up just in time to break up an attack on an ancient Roman two-wheeled carriage with two women and an old man inside.

"Her name is Gracilia, and she was a widow, living in an old villa and struggling to keep the farm going with three slaves."

"She must be very beautiful . . ." said Vortipor, but Guendivar wondered. It had always seemed to her that Gualchmai was so successful with women just because he found *all* of them beautiful.

"She . . ." Gualchmai gestured helplessly, seeking for words. "She is what I need."

She is his Vessel of Light— thought Guendivar as the conversation continued.

"I thought I had made Britannia safe because there were no more enemies attacking from outside her borders," said Artor at last, "but you are not the only one to have encountered worse evil within. My own injuries kept me confined to Camalot for too long. In the future it will be different, I swear."

For three days, after the full of the moon, Morgause lay half conscious and drained of energy. When Doli, concerned because she had not called him in the morning, had gone to her, he had found the Cauldron back in its chest and his mistress lying unconscious beside it. Morgause had no memory of having put it there, but for some time, her memories of the entire night remained fragmented, like something remembered from a dream.

But certain facts remained with her, and as the days passed, they became clearer.

The Cauldron's power was far greater than she had imagined, and far less amenable to human control, and the Isle of Maidens was the only place where it might be safely kept in this world.

The Goddess for whom it was the physical gateway was also greater than Morgause had allowed herself to believe, and the aspects that she had for the past ten years worshipped were no more adequate to represent the whole than the pallid version she had scorned the priestesses of the Isle of Maidens for honoring.

Her mother loved her, and the hostility between them was as much her own fault as it was Igierne's.

When a week had passed and Morgause could stand up without her legs turning to water, she ordered her men to break camp and took the road north towards Luguvalium. They traveled slowly while her strength was returning, and so the moon had grown dark and was beginning to wax once more when they came to the fortress of Voreda.

That night they sheltered in the barracks, abandoned for nearly a century. In the morning, Morgause led the way to the track that wound westward through the hills.

Once, she had known this way well. Now, she took in the prospect revealed by each turn of the road with new eyes. Never before had she been so conscious that this was a place outside ordinary reality, a realm of mountains sculptured by giants, rising like guardians behind the familiar hills. They hid a secret country that she, always so preoccupied by her own concerns, had never really known.

In body Morgause grew steadily stronger. Her past was forgotten, the future unknown. She greeted each dawn with increasing eagerness, wondering what the new day would bring, until they crested the last rise and saw through the black fringe of pine trees a glint of blue.

Where the trail curved round towards the trees stood an ancient boulder. When she had lived here as a child, the maidens used to call it the throne.

Someone was sitting there.

Even before Morgause could see the figure clearly, she sensed who it must be. *Just as my mother knew that I would be coming,* she thought then. *I always believed that we fought because we were too different, but perhaps it was because we are too much the same. . . .*

With a few words she halted Uinuist and Doli. She dismounted, then and took the rein of the pony to whose back the chest had been bound, and started towards the stone.

As she drew closer, Morgause realized that she was not the only one who had changed. She had never believed that her mother could look so fragile. The sunlight that dappled the ground beneath the pine needles seemed to shine through her.

There was another thing. Igierne was a trained priestess, and Morgause had seen her often in the willed and disciplined stillness of ritual. But there had always been a tension, a sense of leashed power in reserve, like a warhorse on a tight rein. Now, her mother simply sat still.

"I have brought the gift of the Goddess back to its place . . ." said Morgause, letting the lead rope fall.

"You do not say that you have brought it back to *me*," observed Igierne.

"It is not yours," said Morgause. "Nor is it mine . . . that is what I have learned."

"If you know that, you have learned a great deal."

"I have indeed . . ." Morgause gave a rather shaky sigh and dropped down to sit cross-legged in the dust at her mother's feet. Through the trees she could see sunlight dancing on the blue water, and knew the Lake for another vessel of power.

Manus was nearly the last of the seekers to come back to Camalot, and when he returned, he rode clad as a warrior, escorting a young priestess who had been sent by Igierne.

"I am glad to see you!" said Guendivar when the babble of welcome had died down. "But what is all this?" she indicated his armor. "You have changed!"

He blushed as everyone turned to look at him once more, but all could see that he wore the gear as one accustomed, not like a kitchen boy who had stripped some armor from a body he found by the road.

"Why did the Lady send *you* to guard her messenger?" wondered someone.

Aggarban pointed the stick upon which he had been leaning at the kitchen boy.

"And why are ye wearing a Votadini plaid?"

"Because it is mine!" snapped Manus, reddening once more. "And you are a blind oaf, brother, that never stooped to *look* at the folk who serve ye, or ye would have recognized me before!"

There was a moment of stunned silence, and then Gualch-mai guffawed with laughter. "Oh indeed, he has ye there, Aggarban. And in truth he does have the look of Goriat, does he not, Gwyhir?"

"Oh, he does, he does—" agreed the second brother, his gaze travelling upward, "but much, much larger. . . ." And then everyone, even Artor, who had finished his conversation with the priestess, began to laugh.

"And he has outdone you all," said the king, "for Goriat has found the Cauldron, or at least brought word of it. That is the message my mother has sent to me. The sacred vessel is safe in its shrine, and the Lady of the Votadini is there as well."

"*Mother?*" exclaimed the three older brothers, amazement stamping their faces with a momentary identity.

"Was it Morgause who stole it, then?" exclaimed Cai amidst a rising babble of speculation.

"The message does not say, and whatever lies between my sister and my mother is their own affair," Artor said repressively.

"If the Cauldron has been found, then all our wandering warriors can come home," Guendivar said then.

"It will not matter," observed Betiver. "Pagan though it was, I think the Cauldron was what the priests mean by a sacrament—an earthly symbol that points the way to something beyond. That was what we saw that night, and that is what they are looking for."

"Perhaps we have been too successful," Cai said ruefully. "When we were constantly in danger from the Saxons or the Irish, men had no time to worry about much beyond their own skins."

"And now they worry about their sins. . . ." Artor sighed.

"Take comfort, my lord. So long as human beings must live in the world, they will need good government, and heaven does not hold the only beauty of which men dream."

For a moment, Betiver's glance touched Guendivar. Then he looked away. But others had followed the motion, and now she stood at the center of all men's gaze. She heard

their thought clearly, though it was not with her physical ears.
"For some, the Vessel of Light is here . . ."

Igierne made her way along the edge of the Lake. Beyond
the farther shore, the humped shapes of the mountains rose
up against the luminous blue of the night sky like a black
wall, shutting out the world. Beyond the lapping of the water
and the crunch of her footsteps on stone and gravel, the night
was still. The surface was uneven and she moved carefully,
using her staff for support, for her stiff joints would not be
able to save her if she should fall. It was one of the disad-
vantages of growing older, and at this moment, she felt both
old and tired.

But for the first time in many moons, she was at peace. Her
daughter had come home as Igierne's own mother had foretold. Morgause had much to unlearn as well as to learn before
the rage and hatred in which she had lived for so many years
were entirely replaced by wisdom and love. Igierne did not
suppose that their relationship would always be peaceful, but
at least they now *had* one, instead of a state of war. And the
Lady of the Lake had no desire to break her daughter's will—
to rule the Isle of Maidens, Morgause would need to be
strong, as she had been strong. But Igierne could foresee,
now, a time when she herself would be able to let go.

The Lake slept beneath the stars, reflecting only an occasional flicker of light, and on the island, the priestesses slept
likewise. Only the Lady of the Lake was still wakeful. On the
eastern point a bench had been set for those who wished to
salute the sun or watch the moonrise. With a sigh Igierne
settled herself upon it and laid down the staff. Her priestesses
came here often when the moon was new or full. But the
waning moon was an old woman who rose late and ruled the
silent hours between midnight and dawn, and she had few
worshippers.

She is like me . . . Igierne smiled to herself. Let Morgause
learn to wield the full moon's power. Her coming had freed
her mother to study the secrets of the waning moon and the
dark, to truly become the raven whose wings shine white in
the Otherworld—Branuen, the Hidden Queen.

As if the thought had been a summons, Igierne glimpsed behind the mountain a pallid glow. In another moment, the Crone's silver sickle appeared in the sky.

"Lady of Wisdom, be welcome," whispered Igierne. "Cut away that which I need no longer, and purify my spirit, until it is time for me to return to your dark Cauldron and be reborn. . . ."

PEOPLE AΠD PLACES

A note on pronunciation:

British names are given in fifth-century spelling, which does not yet reflect pronunciation changes. Initial letters should be pronounced as they are in English. Medial letters are as follows.

SPELLED	PRONOUNCED
p	b
t	d
k/c	(soft) g
b	v (approximately)
d	soft "th" (modern Welsh "dd")
g	"yuh"
m	v

✝

PEOPLE IN THE STORY:

CAPITALS=major character
*=historical personnage
( )=dead before story begins
[ ]=name as given in later literature
Italics=deity or mythological personage

*Aelle, king of the South Saxons

Aggarban [Agravaine]—third son of Morgause

(*Ambrosius Aurelianus—emperor of Britannia and Vitalinus' rival)

(Amlodius, Artor's grandfather)

Amminius—one of Artor's men

ARTOR [Arthur]—son of Uthir and Igierne, High King of Britannia

(Artoria Argantel—Artor's grandmother)

BETIVER [Bedivere]—nephew to Riothamus, one of Artor's Companions

Bleitisbluth—a Pictish chieftain

Brigantia/Brigid—British goddess of healing, inspiration, and the land

CAI—son of Caius Turpilius, Artor's foster-brother and Companion

CATAUR [Cador]—prince of Dumnonia

Cathubodva—Lady of Ravens, a British war goddess

*Catraut, prince of Verulamium

*Ceawlin—son of Ceretic

Ceincair—a priestess on the Isle of Maidens

(*Ceretic [Cerdic]—king of the West Saxons)

*Chlodovechus [Clovis]—king of the Franks in Gallia

*Constantine—son of Cataur

*Cunobelinus—warleader of the northern Votadini

Cunorix—an Irish warleader, formerly Artor's hostage

*Cymen—Aelle's eldest son

Doli—a Pictish warrior in the service of Morgause

*Drest Gurthinmoch—High King of the Picts

Dugech—one of Morgause's women

*Dubricius—bishop of Isca and head of the Church in Britannia

*Dumnoval [Dyfnwal]—lord of the S. Votadini

Ebrdila—an old priestess on Isle of Maidens

Edrit—a young warrior in the service of Aggarban

Eldaul the younger [Eldol]—prince of Glevum

*Eormenric—son of Oesc, child king of Cantuware

Ganeda [Ganiedda]—Merlin's half-sister, wife of Ridarchus

(Gorlosius [Gorlois]—first husband of Igierne, father of Morgause)

Goriat [Gareth]—fourth son of Morgause

Gracilia—wife of Gualchmai

GUALCHMAI [Gawain]—first son of Morgause

GUENDIVAR [Gwenivere]—Artor's queen

Gwyhir [Gaheris]—second son of Margause

Hæthwæge—a wisewoman in the service of Eormanaric

(*Hengest—king of Cantuware, leader of Saxon revolt)

Ia—a priestess on the Isle of Maidens, in service of Morgause

*Icel—king of the Anglians in Britannia

IGIERNE [Igraine]—Artor's mother, Lady of the Lake

*Illan—King of Leinster, who for a time holds part of North Wales

Julia—a nun from the Isle of Glass, Guendivar's companion

Father Kedi—an Irish priest at the court of Artor

Leodagranus [Leoderance]—prince of Lindinis, Guendivar's father

Leudonus [Lot]—king of the Votadini

Leuku—one of Morgause's women

Mother Maduret—abbess of the nuns at the Isle of Glass

Matauc [Madoc]—king of the Durotriges

MEDRAUT [Mordred]—fifth son of Morgause, by Artor

Melguas [Meleagrance]—an Irishman born in Guenet, abductor of Guendivar

MERLIN—druid and wizard, Artor's advisor

MORGAUSE—daughter of Igierne and Gorlosius, queen of the Votadini

Morut—a priestess on the Isle of Maidens

(*Naitan Morbet—king of all the provinces of the Picts)

Nest—a priestess on the Isle of Maidens

Ninive—daughter of Gualchmai by a woman of the hills

(*Oesc—grandson of Hengest and king of Cantuware, Eormenric's father)

Peretur [Peredur]—son of Eleutherius, lord of Eboracum

Petronilla—wife of Leodegranus, Guendivar's mother

*Ridarchus—king at Alta Cluta and protector of Luguvalium

Rigana—widow of Oesc, Eormenric's mother

*Riothamus—ruler of Armorica

Tulach—a Pictish priestess, wife of Blietisbluth

Uinist—a Votadini warrior who serves Morgause

Uorepona—"the Great Mare," High Queen of the Picts

(Uthir [Uther Pendragon]—Artor's father)

(*Vitalinus, the Vor-Tigernus—ruler of Britannia who brought in the Saxons)

✝

PLACES

Afallon [Avalon]—Isle of Apples, Glastonbury

Alba—Scotland

Alta Cluta—Kingdom of the Clyde

Anglia—Lindsey and Lincolnshire

Aquae Sulis—Bath

Belisama Fluvius—River Ribble, Lancashire

Bodotria Aestuarius—Firth of Forth

Britannia—Great Britain

Caledonian forest—southern Scotland

Calleva—Silchester

Camalot [Camelot]—Cadbury Castle, Somerset

Cantium, Cantuware—Kent

Cantuwareburh—Canterbury

Cicutio—Brecon, Wales

Demetia—Pembroke and Carmanthenshire
Durnovaria—Dorchester, Dorset
Fodreu—Fortriu, Fife
Gallia—France
Glevum—Gloucester
Guenet [Gwynedd]—Denbigh and Caernarvonshire
Isle of Glass [Inis Witrin]—Glastonbury
Isle of Maidens, the Lake—Derwentwater, Cumbria
Isca (Silurum)—Caerwent
Lindinis—Ilchester, Somerset
Lindum—Lincoln
Londinium—London
Mona—Anglesey
Sabrina Fluvia—the Severn River and estuary
Segontium—Caernarvon, Wales
Sorviodunum—Old Sarum, Salisbury
Summer Country—Somerset
Urbs Legionis [Deva]—Chester
Uxela Fluvius—River Axe, Severn estuary
Venta Belgarum—Winchester
Venta Siluricum—Caerwent, Wales
Viroconium—Wroxeter
Voreda—Old Penrith, Cumberland